I0527583

Shadow Lane
Volume 6

Put to the Blush

by
Eve Howard

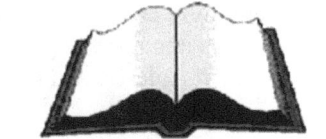

CCB Publishing
British Columbia, Canada

Shadow Lane Volume 6: Put to the Blush,
A Novel of Spanking, Sex and Love

Copyright ©2009 by Eve Howard
ISBN-13 978-1-926585-45-1
Second Edition

Library and Archives Canada Cataloguing in Publication
Howard, Eve, 1953-
Shadow lane volume 6: put to the blush, a novel of spanking, sex and love /
written by Eve Howard – 2nd ed.
ISBN 978-1-926585-45-1
Also available in electronic format.
I. Title.
PS3608.O82S536 2009   813'.6   C2009-904880-9

Cover artwork by Tarsis: www.briantarsis.com
Interior artwork by The Contessa and Tarsis

Shadow Lane Volume 6 was first published by Blue Moon in 2001,
Copyright © Eve Howard.

Publisher: CCB Publishing
               British Columbia, Canada
               www.ccbpublishing.com

Dedicated to

the excellent Fred R.

Crossjay and Teresa

Shadow Lane

Volume 6

Put to the Blush,
A Novel of Spanking, Sex and Love

৪৩

Contents

Sloane and Pamela

Chapter One

Robert and Hazel

It was barely ten o'clock on Monday morning when Robert Corning, publisher of Breathless, Romantic Traveler and Honeymoon, called Hazel Weber, editor of Breathless, into his office.

"You couldn't have done a worse job on this issue!" he declared, slamming the magazine down on his desk in a style that caused Hazel to perceive that this was not to be their usual coffee break.

"I'm sorry," she volunteered immediately. "What was it you didn't like, Mr. Corning?"

"Sit down and I'll tell you," he directed her to a chair by the side of his large conference table and sat down himself. Hazel had never felt her heart pound so violently as when she watched her boss leaf through the company's second most popular magazine with his big hands. "First of all, every story in this issue is narrated by a single woman who manages to have lots of sex without ever getting married, divorced, having kids or contracting a social disease. I'm sure I told you when I hired you, Hazel, that our audience is mostly comprised of young married or divorced moms. How are they going to relate?"

"But tales of domesticity aren't sexy. I think women buy our magazines to escape from their drab reality," Hazel ventured boldly.

"Girl, are you insane? There should be at least two wedding night scenes in every story, the first depicting the author's first, failed honeymoon, and the second describing her second bid for nuptial bliss in the capable arms of a trucker or cowboy who loves her in spite of her hyper-active child."

"I see," Hazel mumbled, barely hearing a word he spoke in her sudden anticipation of being fired. Like most 25 year olds in L.A., she lived from paycheck to paycheck.

"Furthermore, none of the stories you put in this issue contain those endearing characters and heart rending situations that serve to convey positive moral statements about home and family. And you've also been too esoteric. Did you think you were writing for the literati? Are we sitting in the offices of Vanity Fair?" Robert gestured around the faux wood walls of his conference room. "Do you think that if even one of your readers had ever heard of Madame de Stael that they would be reading this type of magazine?" he demanded.

"I guess not," Hazel admitted, now completely convinced that she was about to be dismissed.

"I had my trepidations about hiring a Stanford English major, but you assured me that you understood the simple, basic requirements of writing pulp romance."

"I guess I just thought I was supposed to write about sex without being vulgar."

"I have no complaints about the way you write your sex scenes, it's what surrounds them that's the problem. This is a genre with particular requirements, Hazel, among the most important of which is the reinforcement of solid, sentimental, middle class values. Your stories are too sophisticated. And there's not one tearjerker in the bunch. Don't you understand that you have to pile on the deprivation to make the happy ending seem even happier?"

Hazel did not know what to say and merely waited for him to go on.

"Look Hazel, I'm not saying I don't enjoy your writing personally. But unless you're able to write in a way that reflects the attitudes of our readers, I won't be able to keep you."

"I understand," she said, rising to leave.

"Sit down, I'm not through with you yet," he ordered. "Now tell me something. What's with you and spanking?"

"Excuse me?" Hazel began to blush.

"Three out of five of your stories had spanking scenes. You know, if we want to keep our audience we have to remain politically correct. One spanking per issue is plenty."

"Okay," said Hazel, the blush deepening beautifully.

"Not that I have any personal objection to spanking," he stated bluntly. "In fact, I've a good mind to spank you for the job you did on this issue."

Hazel's fear of being fired was instantly transformed to a butterfly in her tummy. Mr. Corning was gruff and cynical, but he was also only 35, impressively tall and rather handsome.

"I'm very sorry," she said again, almost dizzy with a feeling she had only known through fantasies.

"Next issue, I want to see all the copy before it goes to lay-out."

"I understand."

"Get it to me a week from today. You took far too long with the copy last month and we barely had enough time to set up the photo shoots. You'll have to work fast for awhile to get ahead of your schedule."

"I only have one week?"

"You can do it. Just don't be such a perfectionist. The first idea that comes into your head should be your story. Don't bother refining it so much. Go on to the next job instead."

"I'll try, Mr. Corning."

"Good. I have to get to work now," he dismissed her and began to make his morning phone calls. Hazel tottered to the door in her fitted taupe wool suit and high heels, feeling Robert's gaze upon her until she disappeared.

Once she got back to her office she lit a cigarette and sat back in her chair to construct plots.

She had known three spanking references in one magazine was excessive. But how odd of him to have noticed them! He almost seemed as tuned in to spanking as she was. In fact, he had even expressed the desire to spank her!

Hazel shook her head skeptically. He probably just wanted to add her to his collection of office conquests, and in searching for a hook in her stories he had stumbled on her principal turn-on.

She had heard about Robert's vigorous libido from several of her co-workers. And she could not help but suspect that Ellen Parsons, the perfect blonde editor of Honeymoon, the company's flagship magazine, was in his pocket as often as possible.

Ellen Parsons, who alternately sickened and amused Hazel, was a company girl. Her magazine was always in on time and flawless, each story brimming with pathos and treacle. Furthermore, Ellen was so efficient about turning in her copy that she also had time to cast, schedule, shop for and art direct the photo shoots that illustrated their magazines. To accomplish all of this, Ellen worked over time and gloried in her martyrdom.

Ellen was 31 and unmarried. Maintaining a constant size 2 made her tense. When Hazel joined the team, with her womanly curves, masses of wavy, light brown hair and superior degree, Ellen almost lost her composure. Two months later the girls were not yet friends. And Hazel wondered just how many faults in her magazine had been discovered and revealed to Robert by Ellen.

The week passed in a blur. Whenever Hazel passed Robert in the hall she was overcome by embarrassment, while he virtually ignored her. He seemed to have lost confidence in her and this upset Hazel greatly. It was a strange little job she had landed, but it was as close to a real editorial position as she had come by so far and she felt that in time she could get Robert to remove all or most of the restrictions he'd just placed upon her creativity.

After working at home all weekend on letters and editorials, Hazel arrived at work on Monday morning with her assignment completed, only to find that Robert had gone to Europe and wouldn't be back till the following week.

Hazel spent the week rewriting pieces for the issue she had just turned in, to avoid a second scolding when it came out. She added unhappy marriages, sticky divorces, kids with disabilities, episodes of surgery and chemotherapy, wounding in foreign wars, the pains of relocation and the vicissitudes of trailer park life. She also made sure that four out of five of the narrators prayed fervently to God during all crisis points. Only when she had done all this damage did Hazel feel as though she had saved her job, though it lacerated her soul.

Meanwhile, the idea of receiving a spanking from Robert began to preoccupy her. In one respect, it was too scary to even think about, because her boss was an adult, and a bad tempered one at that. When he walked into a room all conversation ceased until his will was known. His impatience and bluntness of address rendered his workers industrious and meek. Yet everyone liked and respected him.

Robert owned a print shop and bindery as well as the publishing house and had many employees to supervise and provide for. One could never be around him for more than a few minutes without becoming aware of the pressures bearing down on him.

Robert's power frightened rather than attracted Hazel, who was too new in the business to understand his particular genius. Because of his despotic nature, she could never feel truly comfortable in his presence, yet in spite of this, she had recently begun to construct elaborate fantasies involving her boss. Meanwhile, she did her best to stay out of his way.

Spring, and therefore summer, set in early that year in Los Angeles, with temperatures soaring into the upper eighties in the beginning of March. The lilacs in bloom outside Hazel's window at work gave off a heavy, intoxicating perfume as she stood up and stretched in her sundress. It was two o'clock on a Friday afternoon and she decided to run across the street for a cappuccino.

As she crossed the recently gentrified La Brea Avenue, she noticed Robert rapidly consuming a hot dog at Pinks. She pretended not to see him however, lest being spotted by his least favorite editor somehow annoy him.

A minute after she sat down at one of the sidewalk tables in front of the coffee bar, Robert's shadow fell across her blueberry cobbler.

"Hi," he said, falling into the chair opposite her and shaking out a cigarette.

"Oh, hi!" she exclaimed with an accelerated heartbeat.

"I haven't really had a chance to talk to you since I got back from Europe," he began in a friendly tone.

"No." She found herself too embarrassed to meet his eyes. Their casual coffee breaks had ceased on the day he had first taken her to task and she had never willingly entered his office since.

"Ellen tells me you took the trouble to fix up all the copy for the next issue to conform with our guidelines. Thanks for doing that without being told."

"I won't make any more mistakes," she promised.

5

"So tell me, Hazel," he began on a less sober note, "did you put a spanking story in the new issue?"

"Just one."

"I figured you would."

"You said that one would be okay."

"I'll make a point of reading it."

Hazel felt her face grow warm.

"You keep writing spanking stories and I'm going to start thinking that you're into it," he declared, smiling at her sudden disinterest in the tempting cobbler.

"Well, of course I'm into it," she replied, feeling some of the tension leave her shoulders.

"I heard you were over at Augie Rose the other day," said Robert, abruptly switching back to boss mode. He had named an associate publisher. Augie Rose used Robert's print shop and the two CEO's maintained cordial relations. But on more than one occasion Augie had lured good editors and artists away from Corning with higher salaries, a nicer location in Beverly Hills and better benefits. This made Robert feel uneasy about Hazel visiting his place of business.

"Oh, yes, I was meeting my friend for lunch. He's an editor there."

"Hazel, social contacts in the industry are fine things, but please remember that Augie Rose is a competitor," he told her firmly. Hazel didn't quite understand what he was getting at, but instantly realized that accepting the freelance assignment from Augie Rose had been unwise.

"How did you know I was over there?" Hazel casually asked him.

"Oh, Ellen was picking up some discs and saw you."

Hazel inserted her fork into her cobbler without taking a bite. How like Ellen to have snitched.

"They haven't made you an offer, have they? Tell me the truth," he demanded.

"Offer?"

"Of an in-house editorship."

"Oh no!" she replied immediately. With any luck she would not have to admit she'd accepted the freelance.

"Good. Are you going to eat that?"

"I guess I'm not really hungry," she said truthfully. Robert relieved her of the dessert and dispatched it rather quickly.

"Thanks," he told her, getting up and drifting back across the street to work.

Now Hazel was in a quandary. She wanted to keep the free lance from Augie Rose, but knew that if Robert found out about it he would be displeased. And with Ellen around he would not go long in ignorance. Ellen lunched with Augie Rose employees once or twice a week and it was obvious that she was Robert's spy.

All the rest of the afternoon Hazel sat distracted at her desk, revolving the idea of confessing to Robert at once. It was still early enough in her career at Corning to plead ignorance of the rules.

Finally, at four-thirty, Robert himself took a stroll through the building, telling everyone that they could leave early.

"Hey, get out of here," he said, sticking his head into Hazel's small office.

"Robert?" her timid plea for attention brought him in.

"Yes, Hazel?"

"May I talk to you for a minute?"

"Sure, what's on your mind?" He came in and sat on the edge of her worktable while she kept her seat at her desk.

"It's about Augie Rose."

"Yes? What about Augie Rose?" His rather broad (she'd been noticing lately) shoulders stiffened and he folded his arms across a chest still pristinely clothed in a starched shirt and silk foulard tie.

"Well, I guess I didn't really understand the company policy with regard to other publishers and I accepted some free lance from Augie Rose."

"What kind of free lance?" he frowned.

"The letters section for the July issue of Bridal Romance."

"How much are they paying you?"

"$350 for six thousand words," she mumbled.

"That's more than I'd pay," he declared.

"Is there a rule against accepting outside freelance?"

"Of course."

"Oh."

"Did you already turn in the job?"

"I promised it to them for Monday."

"Hazel, you should have known better," he accused.

"I'm really sorry," Hazel submissively replied.

"Have you accepted any more assignments?"

"No."

"Well, see that you don't."

"I won't."

"Aren't you getting paid enough?"

"Yes, but you know how it is," she tried to explain.

"We can give you free lance just as well as Augie Rose. Meanwhile I'd rather your talents not be employed in the aid of my main competitor."

"I'm really sorry I broke the rules," Hazel said sincerely.

"Just don't do it again."

"I won't," she repeated. He looked at her thoughtfully for a moment, then shook his head to clear it of a dangerous thought before drifting out of the room. Hazel subsided in her seat with a sigh, her heart thumping. That wasn't so bad, she thought to herself. He hadn't even raised his voice. And he'd offered her free lance, though at a lower rate than Augie Rose.

She began to stuff her purse with her belongings and run a brush through her hair when Robert marched abruptly back into her office.

"I've just been thinking, Hazel, you committed two major errors in one month," he said, pushing a straight-backed chair into the center of the floor. "If I don't correct you now, who knows what you might do next," he told her, sitting squarely on the chair and patting his trousered thigh. "Come over here, young lady."

Hazel stared at him wide eyed.

"Don't keep me waiting, Hazel," he snapped.

"You're teasing me," Hazel protested, blushing fiercely.

"Think so?" Robert got up, captured her bare upper arm in a very firm grip, pulled her out of her chair and had her across his lap in a moment. "There," he said, smoothing out the snug, straight skirt of her 50's style summer dress, "Does this feel like I'm teasing?" Smack! His large hand nearly covered her right cheek as it connected with a resounding spank.

"No!" she cried, shocked and transported by the first slap of his palm on her firm, tautly skirted bottom.

Robert smacked her again, on the left cheek, with a loud report. It had begun so quickly that Hazel barely had time to catch her breath. Now ticklish tremors exploded inside her like bolts of liquid light.

He immediately began to spank her through her skirt with his well-padded hand. Supported by his broad, muscular thighs and held in place by his hand on her waist, Hazel did not attempt escape. For every time his hand came down a palpable thrill shot through her. So this was what a spanking really felt like! No wonder the act haunted her thoughts.

Robert smacked her firmly and rhythmically, on the right cheek, then the left, starting slowly, then gradually quickening the tempo. She counted four sets of twelve before he paused to rub away the sting. Even through her skirt and panties, the spanking penetrated deeply and her bottom felt radiant.

Observing the way she wriggled and arched to his hand, Robert continued administering the discreet but very sound spanking to his editor, warming the entire surface of her elegant, oval bottom through her linen dress. He went on spanking her until his arm got tired, which took quite a long time. Even though he spanked her hard, her dress and panties softened the blows and rendered them entirely erotic to the enchanted Hazel. Even so, Robert was determined that Hazel feel thoroughly spanked before he let her go.

When he released her, her legs nearly gave out under her as waves of excitement still coursed through her tummy and contracted her heart.

"Aren't you going to thank me for not pulling up your skirt?" he asked.

"Thank you," she said, timidly, rubbing her bottom through her skirt, then added mischievously, "I think."

"I decided to be lenient, since it was your first time."

"How did you know that?"

"Never mind. I know a lot of things. For example, I know about every type of mischief a girl can get up to around here, and I'll be keeping a sharp eye on you from now on."

Hazel felt quite startled to realize that she had finally received corporal punishment from a true enthusiast in command of language as correct as his form. Hazel gazed at him with blunt admiration and Robert looked pleased with himself.

"You know, you're very sexy," he told her as he went out the door. The freshets of pleasure continued to wash through her as she gathered up her things and left the office.

The deliriously perfumed dry heat of a Santa Ana wind ruffled the split in her skirt as Hazel waited at the bus stop a few minutes later. So enraptured was she with the memory of her spanking that she didn't notice Robert roar up to the curbside on his huge Harley. She had never seen him on his bike before and he had to lift the helmet before she recognized him with a start.

"Where do you live?" he demanded.

"Just over in West Hollywood," she replied, with a freshly pounding heart.

"Get on and I'll give you a ride," he told her, handing her the extra helmet.

"But, my skirt–" she began.

"— has a slit – hike it up and you should have no problem getting on," he advised her, taking her purse and shoving it into a side bag. The hog was huge and had been modified to fit all the requirements of a 6'5" millionaire. As monumental as man and machine then appeared, Hazel could not contemplate roaring down the hill into West Hollywood on the back of the Harley with anything less than sheer terror. Nevertheless, she got on the back of the bike and locked her arms around Robert's trim waist.

"I thought you had a car," he said, kick-starting his machine.

"It recently died," she explained. A second later they were out in traffic and darting in between cars. La Cienega came all too soon and Hazel prepared for her worst scare since the earthquake. But strangely, the hill simply seemed to disappear obediently under the wheels of the bike without simulating a roller coaster ride in the slightest. Hazel began to relax her grip slightly on Robert's waist and by the end of the ride, four minutes later, at the quiet, residential intersection of Croft and Waring Streets, she had almost begun to enjoy herself.

Hazel dismounted as gracefully as she could, accepted her purse and handed him the helmet.

"Well, I suppose you'll be starting your free lance job now," he said disapprovingly. Hazel immediately blushed as she realized that he was as reluctant to leave her as she was to see him go.

"I'm very sorry about that," she reiterated sincerely.

"I should have spanked you harder for that," he grumbled. Hazel merely looked at him with wide eyes. "And longer," he added, looking sexier straddling the powerful motorcycle than any character she had ever created to fuel her fantasies. Why had it taken her months to realize that a virility god ruled her workplace? Why hadn't she noticed the vee that was formed by his shoulders and waist? Or that Roman coin head which sat so nobly atop his columnar neck?

"I can still feel it," she told him.

"I'll bet it isn't even pink," he declared.

"I'll bet it is," she replied.

"Lift up your skirt and show me," he told her casually. Now her blush grew even deeper.

"No!"

Robert laughed and said, "Will you have dinner with me tomorrow?"

A tremor went through Hazel as she realized that a courtship of sorts had begun. "Oh, yes!" she said, looking up at her apartment with indecision. She couldn't bear to let him go like this, when her empty apartment contained so many straight-backed chairs, sofas, hairbrushes, etc., to furnish them with pleasure. Robert saw her eyes go to the windows and looked at her questioningly.

"Is someone waiting for you?"

"No. I live alone," she replied, helpfully.

"May I see?"

"Yes."

Robert parked the bike and followed her up a brick staircase to a second floor apartment in a pretty little Tudor-style building. Leaded glass windows and hardwood floors had made this space a heavenly find and Hazel had used a small inheritance to furnish it. Her resources impressed Robert.

He examined her recamier with interest then looked her up and down.

"How tall are you?" he asked.

"Five-seven."

This admission caused Robert to go in search of a larger sofa, which he found in her living room. This was where he elected to sit down and be served tea.

"When did you first start thinking about spanking?" he asked her.

"Age three."

"For me it was six."

"So you're really into it," she marveled.

"I don't think you could find someone who was any more into it," Robert confessed.

"You respond to those scenes in old movies?"

"Tell me your favorites and I'll tell you mine," he challenged.

"Okay. For me it has to be Frontier Gal, Professional Sweetheart and Captain Lightfoot."

"You have exquisite taste. Mine would be Too Young To Kiss, The Battle of The Villa Florita and The Cave of Memories."

So he enjoyed juvenile fantasies! This was becoming more deliciously decadent by the moment.

"I'd love to own a pair of ruffled rumba panties," she mused, referring to a scene in one of the films he had mentioned, "but where does one find them?" she wondered, wildly exhilarated at finally discussing this subject freely and in detail with a knowledgeable, sympathetic male.

"They sell them at Dream Dresser. I'll buy you some," Robert promised.

"You will?"

"Speaking of movies, have you ever seen any really good spanking movies?"

"There are specific spanking movies?" she asked, amazed.

"Oh, hundreds. I think I own them all. I've been collecting since the days of Super Eight."

"Are they good?"

"I'll show you some and you can tell me."

"I feel like I'm dreaming," said Hazel.

"How do you think I felt when, idly looking over your galleys, I came across not one but three spanking stories seeded into the magazine? One or two references might be coincidental or unconscious, but three?"

"Do you think other people will notice?"

"Only others of our kind. To return to my tender recollection, I've actually been waiting for several weeks for the opportunity to discipline you." His pointed use of their favorite word made her color yet again. "Your confession today seemed to provide that opportunity," Robert continued. "Normally, I don't flirt with my employees, but because of our mutual interest, I felt you might welcome the attention."

"I'm sure you could see how the spanking affected me."

"I did seem to notice you not protesting when I first turned you over my knee."

"But, don't you have a girlfriend that you spank?" she asked shyly, trying to ignore the rush of pleasure that went through her every time he chanced to utter a potent phrase.

"I go to B&D clubs and play pretty regularly but I have no girlfriend."

"After you read my stories, what did you think?"

"I thought, 'She's into it, she's brilliant and she works for me. I've got to find a reason to spank her.'"

"Were you looking for one all this time?"

"Oh, you don't know," he laughed. "I've been clocking your arrival to the minute every morning and I've got my little Ellen monitoring your lunches and breaks. I must say you've been annoyingly punctual these past two weeks."

"Do you spank your little Ellen too?" Hazel ventured.

"No way in hell," he replied. "She doesn't know a thing about this stuff and we're going to keep it that way."

"Don't look at me, I never talk to her if I can avoid it."

"Do I detect a lack of sympathy between you and Ellen?"

"No, sir."

"Ellen may be a pill but she produces and that makes me happy."

"Ellen is a model employee," Hazel agreed.

"She's loyal, which is more than I can say for you, running over to Augie Rose!" Robert suddenly seemed to remember why he came up to Hazel's apartment.

"But I had no idea that I was doing wrong. I just needed the money."

"Ignorance is no excuse in the eyes of the law," he reminded her.

"Are you the law?"

"At work I am."

"What's a B&D club?"

"That's a place where men go to do spanking sessions with professional ladies."

"So, whenever you want to spank a girl, you just go there?"

"That's what I've been doing."

"And these women who get the spankings, are they into it?"

"Some are."

"Is sex involved?"

"Not in the sessions I've done."

"Are they pretty, these women?"

"Some are."

"What do they charge?"

"Why are you so interested?"

"I can't conceive of it being my job to get spankings."

"Hazel, get that starry look out of your eyes. There's nothing glamorous about working in a B&D parlor."

"Oh? I'll bet the girls you see get pretty excited when you walk in the door. The ones that are into it, I mean."

"Maybe there is a slight touch of glamour to the dungeon," Robert conceded reflectively, "but there's a tawdry and dangerous side to it too." He looked at her sternly. "Don't even think about moonlighting that way, Hazel."

Hazel was unconscious of the pout that suddenly came to her beautiful mouth, for she had already made the leap in her mind to working in a dungeon.

"Oh, god no!" she quickly demurred.

"If you're really curious about what clubs are like, I'll take you with me to one and you can study the atmosphere."

Hazel considered this prospect.

"Well, Hazel, I think it's time," he said, putting down his teacup. The next thing she knew, he had pulled her across his lap. His thighs were like a marble cloud beneath her, infinitely seductive and strong. As he curved his hand around her waist to hold her in position, she was overcome by flutters. Was it to be like this every time he took hold of her?

This time he pushed her skirt up to her narrow waist. Her legs were bare and she wore sheer white nylon panties. This first actual glimpse of Hazel's perfect bottom nearly took Robert's breath away. He had known her shape was divine from the tight suit skirts she wore, but now he could observe that the texture of her bisque skin was also flawless.

"Now you're gonna get it," he warned her, rolling up his sleeves. Catching their reflection in the long mirror over the fireplace, Hazel watched him prepare to spank her with rapturous anticipation. The determination with which he raised his arm to administer the first smack gave her a thrill that persisted throughout the entire spanking.

Robert began to rain sharp, stinging smacks down upon her upturned bottom.

"Ow!" She squirmed and wriggled. This was starting fast! Then suddenly he stopped spanking and instead stroked the sting away. He massaged her till she arched to his hand. Only then did he resume the spanking. Alternating from cheek to cheek, he delivered full-bodied smacks, in response to which, Hazel whimpered and moaned. Then, just as her bottom was becoming radiantly warm, he again ceased spanking and commenced soothing her tender, pink flesh. Only this time, he also placed his palm against the crotch of her panties to press against her pussy and feel how wet she had become. Robert kept one hand firmly on the curve of her waist while he punished and caressed her.

Hazel was on fire. Never had a man paid such attentions to her.

Each time he returned to spanking, however, he seemed to spank a little bit harder. Hazel abandoned herself and very nearly sobbed, though the pain was far from unbearable. It was that he was such a big man. Hazel felt as vulnerable as a child across his knee and this evoked decades of forbidden fantasies. She had longed for a big man forever.

Robert warmed her panties for twenty minutes, tingeing her bottom magenta with the palm of his hand. This treatment caused her to squirm across his lap in rapturous discomfort. But before the much anticipated moment of having her panties pulled down and being entirely exposed arrived, Robert's pager beeped.

"That's probably the print shop," he told her, gently pulling her up to a sitting position. "Where's your phone?"

Hazel mutely gestured to the end table at his side and he made his call. In a moment he turned to her and reported that he had to go look at the blue line for Honeymoon. Hazel walked him to the door. As they parted on the threshold neither seemed to know how to conclude the encounter. Then Hazel impulsively threw her arms around him and hugged him. His arms immediately closed around her and they stood in the doorway for some time holding on to each other.

Finally Robert broke away and told her, "Don't forget about dinner tomorrow night," then went quickly down the stairs.

Twenty-five minutes later a knock came on Hazel's door. She opened it to a delivery boy bearing two dozen peachy pink roses from Robert. With this she entirely melted. The card, which read, "Try to be good till we meet again," was immediately pressed between the leaves of her journal. The roses were placed on the table by her bed. She stared at her bottom in the mirror for several minutes, admiring the pinkness through her sheer white panties.

"What have you been up to since I saw you last?" Robert asked Hazel on the way to dinner at The Ivy the next night.

"Well, last night and most of today I worked on my free lance," she replied truthfully, half-hoping to rekindle his indignation.

"Humph!" Robert snorted, "I'd almost forgotten about that. Thanks for reminding me, though. I'll give me a good excuse to take a heavy strap to you later tonight at The Keep."

"The Keep? What's that?"

"One of those B&D clubs you were so curious about. I called and made an appointment to occupy one of the dungeons at ten."

"Dungeon sounds so sinister."

"It's just an atmospheric playroom."

"And a heavy strap? For me?"

"You're a big girl, you can take it."

"I'm sure I can't," Hazel protested.

"Just do your best and I'll be happy."

Hazel sat in the parlor of The Keep, waiting for Robert to return from conferring with Mistress Hildegarde about the dungeon. The other occupants of the sitting room were a creamy, little 21-year-old blonde in a white corset, and a sleek, 30 year old brunette in a black leather dress. The woman smoked and answered the phone while the girl painted her nails pale pink, occasionally bouncing up to talk to a client.

The doorbell rang while Hazel was waiting and the pixie went to answer it. She returned with a customer in tow, a big, boyish, ex-football player, about 38, with a thick moustache and gleaming blue eyes.

"So, did you want to see a dominant or a submissive?" the bubbly girl, whose name was Cherry asked.

"Submissive," the man replied, smiling at Hazel hopefully, even though she was clad in a linen dress and jacket rather than fetish attire. Hazel flushed at the desire in the big man's eyes as he appraised her tailored outfit. "Are you available?" he asked her. "I just want to do a light bondage session."

"Me?" Hazel shook her head with a smile. "Oh, no!"

"That's too bad, you'd be perfect," the client commented regretfully.

"What's your fantasy?" Hazel impulsively asked.

"You're a job applicant," the client eagerly explained, "and during the interview I overpower you, tie you to a chair and unbutton your blouse."

"That's it?"

"If you'd permit it, I'd pull up your skirt to expose your stocking top."

"No spanking?"

"Oh, I'd never strike a woman."

"But I'm into spanking," she teased him, eyeing the magnificent thighs straining against his levis.

The sudden entrance of Robert into the room precluded further discourse between Hazel and the broad shouldered client, who looked wistfully after her as Robert took her by the hand and led her upstairs.

"What were you doing talking to that man?" Robert demanded as soon as he shut the door behind them in the blue room known as "Willie," because of the Sweet Gwendolyn drawings, which hung, matted and framed on the walls.

"He wanted to do a session with me," she reported, wandering about the room and examining the various pieces of equipment.

"I hope you undeceived him as to your reason for being here."

"Actually, we made a date for later."

"Don't get smart with me, young lady."

"Why shouldn't I? I'm going to be punished anyway."

"You're damned right you're getting punished. Now go out in the hall and pick a paddle off the wall," Robert instructed while removing his jacket.

Hazel exited the room and returned to the large bank of corporal punishment equipment and restraints she had passed on the way in. Coming up the stairs at the same time were Cherry and the client who had wanted to tie Hazel to a chair.

Suddenly possessed by an imp of misguided mischief, Hazel boldly confronted the pair.

"Oh!" said she, "it's that handsome man from the parlor with the fascinating fantasy. Are you sure you wouldn't like to trade partners with me?" This last remark was addressed directly to Cherry.

"Huh?" said the girl.

"Mr. C. is just a spanking session," said Hazel, then added with sudden inspiration, "and a very good tipper." She had no idea whether the girls ever received tips at the club, but had noted Robert's generosity to their waitress at The Ivy and assumed that his spanking surrogates would also benefit from his largess. "And, I've never been tied up in all my life," she aimed this provocative comment at the client, who was, of course, in favor of Hazel from the start, not only because of her beauty, but because of the outfit she wore.

"Are you sure it's okay with your master?" Cherry queried cautiously.

"Oh, he's not my master," Hazel laughed.

"Let's do it!" the client suddenly said, grabbing Hazel by the hand and pulling her into the red dungeon known as "Munchausen" because of the Edvard Munch vampire reproductions on the walls.

Hazel's heart was pounding violently as the client closed the door – on which there was no lock – behind them and explained what he wanted.

Hazel was extremely shocked that the door did not burst open one, two or three minutes later to reveal a highly irritated Robert, but Hazel and her mock rapist were left alone to play undisturbed.

The session was easy and instructive. First Hazel demanded to examine the contents of the gym bag he'd brought into the dungeon. It held only some neatly coiled white nylon rope. Then the man began to interview her, as though she were a job applicant. She had no trouble adapting to this role. Then suddenly, as she was framing an answer to his second or third bland question, he sprang at her and simply pushed her shoulders back against the chair.

Hazel looked at him in great surprise and tried to seem frightened, though the big teddy bear of a man inspired anything but apprehension in her bosom.

He pulled four equal lengths of white nylon rope out of his bag and quickly tied her wrists to the chair frame behind her and her ankles to its legs. Her a-line skirt allowed her legs to be spread. The man made no motion to gag her, and she began to make token protests against the assault. The man said nothing, but breathed heavily as he unbuttoned the three chunky buttons, which topped her dress and exposed the upper portion of her bosom in its lacy bra. He barely touched her breasts, but seemed to admire them greatly as his large cock came out of his pants and into his hand.

Presently the man exposed the tops of Hazel's gartered stockings, by pulling her skirt up as promised. Still he tugged on his thickening penis, mesmerized by her beauty as she wriggled and strained in the chair without disturbing her bonds in the slightest.

"I insist you release me at once! These ropes are very tight!" Hazel cried, seventeen minutes into the session and completely caught up in her captor's passion. Her phrasing gave the rope man joy and the organ in his grip began to gush a liquid tribute to her charms.

She waited patiently to be untied, which was accomplished in a moment. The client then fell to his knees beside her and respectfully kissed the back of her hand.

"You're adorable, wonderful!" he told her, pressing forty dollars into her hand. In less than two minutes Hazel was downstairs in the main parlor looking for Robert.

Hildegarde, the young mistress of the house, was there with Cherry and both appeared full of concern for their creative new guest. Hildegarde was a strapping auburn-haired Valkyrie of 25, flush with beauty, warmth and wit.

"Okay, gorgeous, here's the story," said Hildegarde, putting her arms around Hazel's shoulders, "he's left and he's mad."

"Left? But didn't he play with Cherry?" Hazel had expected anything but being abandoned at the house.

"Actually, he declined that pleasure," said Hildegarde wryly, comparing the proud carriage and elegant demeanor of her guest with the squeezable cuteness of her employee. "Though he did provide her with allowance to assuage her disappointment at missing a session with "Ken the Rapist"."

"I guess this belongs to you too," said Hazel, proffering the forty dollars Ken had given her.

"No, sweetheart, that's your tip. And here's $30 from the house," Hildegarde said, handing Hazel the additional allowance.

"But I didn't do it for the money," Hazel protested.

"You're going to need cab fare," Hildegarde reminded her. Just then the phone rang and Cherry ran for it. She looked at them immediately with excitement and covering the receiver said, "It's Robert. He's calling from his car. He wants to know if she's still here."

Hazel ran for the phone with a painfully throbbing heart.

"Robert?"

There was a tangible silence. She repeated his name and he finally spoke.

"I've been driving around trying to figure out whether you're crazy, stupid or the most recklessly promiscuous girl I've ever met."

"Stupid is the correct answer," she replied in all humility. "I was just being cute. I never thought you'd let me go through with it. Then once it started, it didn't seem convenient to stop until it was over."

"Is that an excuse or an apology?"

"A most abject apology!" she declared, sensing him soften imperceptibly.

"Good, because there can be no possible logical reason for what you did."

"I know. Now that I think about it, it makes no sense even to me. But all the same, I wish you would come and pick me up."

"You've got money in your pocket, take a cab home!" he hung up huffily. Hazel sighed and put down the phone.

"I really can't explain why I did it," Hazel confessed to Hildegarde as Cherry was made to call the cab. "Except as a way of being a brat."

"You want to watch that sort of thing with someone like Robert. I've observed that he's not a patient man," Hildegarde said. "Where did he find you anyway?"

"I work for him. I'm his most junior editor."

Just then there was a honk outside the window. Cherry bounced over and reported that Robert was waiting outside in his BMW convertible.

"Would you cancel the cab for me?" Hazel asked Hildegarde in a rush as she ran out the door to the street. He opened the door from the inside and said nothing when she got in. Hazel was afraid that he would take her straight home and her heart was pounding violently as they turned up Laurel Canyon Boulevard and began to climb into the hills instead. After turning off the heavily wooded canyon road and threading their way up a series of steep, narrow lanes, they finally arrived at Robert's modest hilltop mansion.

"I got it as a fixer-upper," he explained ushering her inside. "I've probably put more into this place than I paid for it."

"No wonder Corning can't afford to pay as much for free lance as Augie Rose. You've got big expenses," Hazel observed impertinently.

Because he still hadn't stopped being her boss, Robert stared at her incredulously.

"You'd better not be so fresh, young lady," he warned her, "you're already in enough trouble."

"I'm terribly sorry about what I did," she explained, following him through various rooms of the house as he threw his jacket down, picked up his mail, put food down for his slim, grey tabby cat, and came to rest in the dining room with its big oak table and wood beamed ceiling.

"Sit there," he motioned her to a chair, just as though they were back at his conference table at work. She meekly took the seat indicated and gave him her attention, except for gazing distractedly about her now and then to observe the fittings of the room. In a moment the cat jumped up on the table and then into Hazel's lap. Hazel was charmed and caressed it.

"Now tell me again exactly why you did what you did tonight."

"To get in trouble I suppose."

"Oh? Did you honestly think that I couldn't come up with a reason for spanking you all by myself?"

"I didn't think at all. My actions were hasty and ill-judged and I repent them most sincerely."

"Tell me about the session," he demanded, leaning back in his chair and shaking out a cigarette. He threw the pack and lighter across the table to her and she gratefully lit up. The cat wisely jumped off her lap and ran out of the room. Hazel described the session as Robert rose and paced. Presently he spoke.

"You enjoyed it, didn't you?"

"I was curious about bondage," she replied evasively.

"Don't you think you chose a decidedly untimely moment to satisfy your curiosity?"

"Yes, sir."

"That was about the rudest behavior I've ever experienced on a first date, or any other date, for that matter!" Robert declared in a tone that made her tremble. "Can I expect something like this every time we're out together?"

"No, sir," Hazel lowered her eyes.

"I still can't understand how a girl who hasn't even had her first bare bottom spanking yet could make the leap to slutting it in a dungeon with a stranger."

"I can't understand that either," she admitted.

"So I'm to believe that you only did it to get a rise out of me?" He leaned against the sideboard with folded arms.

"I was just being naughty."

Robert frowned at her foolishness but began to unbend.

"What am I going to do with you?" he asked in a tone of resignation, fairly satisfied by now that Hazel was neither insane or a slut but simply an inexperienced player who had acted thoughtlessly in the good cause of provoking a spanking. Hazel made no reply but looked as though she were about to burst into tears. "You deserve to be punished severely," he declared.

"I do?" A spasm gripped her.

"Don't you think you do?"

"I don't know what you mean by severely."

Robert didn't answer immediately but instead poured a shot of bourbon into a glass.

"Drink?" he asked. Hazel shook her head, remembering her two plus glasses of wine at dinner. Perhaps they were partially to blame for her lack of circumspection at the club. "For what you did," he said at length, "you should be made to submit to a spanking and an enema."

Hazel's eyes widened. "An enema? That you give me?" It suddenly seemed very warm in the room.

"Who else?"

"But that's so intimate, so sexual."

"That's what will make it a memorable punishment."

Hazel almost smiled but forced herself to remain sober. "I could never submit to that from you. I would die of embarrassment."

"I'm happy to hear there's still something that embarrasses you," he commented, taking her by the hand and leading her out of the dining room and up the stairs to the master bedroom, which was a large loft.

Although smitten with lust and dumbstruck with self-consciousness, Hazel could not fail to hoot at the colossal, rough-hewn oaken furniture, which decorated the space.

"What?" he demanded.

"Was the Jolly Green Giant having a yard sale?"

"Very amusing. We'll see how witty you are when I finally pull those panties down," he tossed over one shoulder as he searched through massive wardrobes and bureaus for equipment.

"Robert, you weren't serious about the "E" thing, were you?"

"Sure I was." He displayed a boxed Anal Invader kit with satisfaction.

"What are you doing with that stuff?"

"I went to the Pleasure Chest while you were finishing your session, just in case I should have the opportunity to punish you for your insolence tonight."

"But, this is all so intimate," she repeated.

"Damn it, Hazel, why shouldn't we be intimate?" He made her sit beside him on the bench at the foot of the bed.

"Well, for one thing, I'm not even sure that you like me."

"I more than like you."

"But these objects seem so invasive, so sexual. And we hardly know each other. You haven't even kissed me yet," she protested.

Robert kissed her and observed, "These prudish protests don't match the girl who was willing to go into a dungeon with a stranger and let him jack off on her just an hour ago."

"Not on me, in the air! And it was really quite different than what you're proposing. After all, he barely touched me and my genitals were never exposed, no less penetrated repeatedly!" Hazel eyed the Anal Invader set.

"So that made the whole thing pure, did it?"

"Decidedly!"

"You know, I think it's high time I paddled some of the nonsense out of you!" he declared and pulled her across his lap. "The first thing you have to learn," he told her, bringing his big hand down hard on the seat of her skirt, "is that when you're out on a first date with a dominant man, he's the one to decide the evening's agenda!"

Robert did not hesitate this time in pulling up her skirt and pulling down her panties almost immediately. Her bare bottom was pristine save for the red mark his first smack left.

"Ow!"

"It's almost too pretty to spank," he admitted, stroking the spot where his palm had struck.

"Does that mean I can go now?"

Robert began to soundly spank her.

"So you thought it would be cute to interrupt our date in order to pick up a stranger and play with him while palming off Cherry on me! I still can't get over the fact that you thought all of that up yourself."

"I'm a self-starter," she explained, and was rewarded with a series of much harder smacks.

"You know, you put me in a very awkward position," Robert told her, "I had no intention of playing with Cherry, but I still had to pay her for her time after you stepped in and stole her session."

"But, I never thought you'd let it get that far," she explained.

"Well, if it had been a spanking person in that dungeon I never would have, but once I found out about your client's fantasy I decided it would teach you a lesson to have to carry through with your idiotic plan and actually finish the scene. Now get up," he told her, satisfied that he had pinkened her bottom sufficiently for a few minutes, "and go and stand in the corner."

"But –"

"No arguments, young lady. You've been a very bad girl and you need to think about how sorry you are." Robert took her by the upper arm and placed her in the corner, with her panties still pulled down to her knees. She looked momentarily rebellious but he subdued her with a look and she turned to the wall with a pout.

"Hazel?"

"Yes?"

"What are you going to do right now?"

"Think about how sorry I am," she replied, rubbing her glowing bottom.

"That was just your warm up," he informed her. "There's more to come."

Robert disappeared into another room for several minutes. Eventually Hazel pulled up her panties and wandered out of the corner and around the room. When Robert came back in he seemed displeased to find her at large.

"Disobeying me already?"

"But I didn't –" she wasn't able to finish her sentence because Robert caught her around the waist, turned her under his arm and proceeded to administer six stinging smacks to the back of her skirt.

"Ow!" she protested.

"I can see you aren't the slightest bit sorry for what you did tonight," he said, letting her go and deliberately rolling up his sleeves.

"I am," she protested, once again rubbing her bottom. "I wouldn't really make you angry for the world."

"Lose the dress," he ordered, disappearing back into the other room, which she followed him into shortly, while unbuttoning her dress.

The beautifully designed bathroom adjoining his bedroom was the biggest she had ever seen, with skylights in the pitched roof that revealed the full moon through the boughs.

An oversized white enamel claw footed tub stood in the center of the room with a wooden towel rack to one side. The cabinetry was a blend of golden brown and black woods. The walls were painted a smoky blue and offset by polished wooden wainscoting. The primary objects of interest to Hazel were the gray leather massage table and heavy wooden straight-backed chair, which each airily dominated a different portion of the room. The commode and shower were enclosed in separate closets off the main room. Molded candle sconces on the walls held big, cream candles, which Robert lit after dimming the overheads.

She watched him remove an enema apparatus from its plastic bag. "Come on, Hazel," he said, looking up to observe her eyes widen, "admit that you're intrigued."

"I do admit that. But that doesn't mean I feel comfortable about what you're proposing."

"You're not supposed to feel comfortable about it. Just the opposite. It's going to be uncomfortable."

"I suppose you know what you're doing."

"We'll find out, won't we?"

Hazel stepped out of her dress to reveal a Venus body in Christian Dior lingerie. Robert couldn't help but stare at the perfection of her high, round bosom.

"Turn around, darling," he said, to admire the elegant view from the rear. She had a beautiful back that tapered to a slim waist. Her hips flared only slightly. The lace briefs sculpted her oval cheeks. She wore 4" heeled sandals, which revealed her cherry red toenails and made her legs look even longer.

"I'm beginning to see where you get your confidence," Robert commented. She winked at him over one shoulder. "I'm also beginning to see that you're a little flirt!" he declared sternly. "Come over here," he said, seating himself on the armless chair.

"Are you going to spank me again?"

"Certainly I am. Why else would you be here?"

"But not the other thing?"

"Your enema? We'll get to that."

Hazel came to him and let him pull her down across his lap again.

"Why did you pull these back up?" Smack!

"I just did."

"I can see that." A series of hard smacks followed. "You have to learn to be more obedient." He pulled her panties off entirely.

"That's a silly thing to learn to be."

"Not around me, it isn't."

"But, are you my boss now, or something else?"

"Tonight let's just say I'm your dominant."

Hazel savored this as his hand came down. She knew that she was being spanked hard, but her excitement at being across his lap again had risen to such a pitch that it scarcely hurt. Although the sting was building and her skin was beginning to glow.

"You want me to be your dominant, don't you, Hazel?"

"Yes!"

"Except you don't know what that means," he paused to rub the sting away. Then he unhooked her bra and relieved her of it. Now she wore only her high-heeled shoes while every other inch of her smooth, young skin was bare. "A girl is supposed to respect and obey her dominant," he told her.

"I respect you. And I'll try to obey you," she promised.

"You know, Hazel, I didn't appreciate the way you took control tonight, putting major actions into motion that effected me as much as they did you, without even consulting me."

"I didn't think of it like that," she said over one shoulder.

"Put your head down," he told her, deliberately separating her thighs. "You did take control," he repeated, smacking her hard on either cheek, then separating her legs a little more. Hazel's heartbeat accelerated as she realized that he was going to touch her at any moment.

"Okay," she breathed, "you're right, I took control. But just because I didn't know any better."

He rubbed her bottom in circles. Then he spread her legs again and pressed his hand against her sex.

"Hazel, will you obey me for the rest of the evening?"

"Yes."

"And submit to a lesson in self-control?"

"I'll submit," Hazel returned, extremely eager to experience all he had threatened.

"You know, Hazel, there's a lot more to over the knee discipline than just spanking," he told her, spreading her cheeks. "There's the embarrassment of being exposed, as well as the humiliation of being punished anally." Now he lightly spanked the area he spread. "Don't you find this embarrassing, Hazel?"

"Yes!" she managed to utter between whimpers.

"Let me examine you," he said, pulling her cheeks well apart. She held her breath as he held her spread, then spanked her bottom hole again, harder this time.

"Oh!" she cried softly, for it felt sexy and her clit had begun to ache.

"Don't you need to be punished like this Hazel?" Robert asked, giving her one last chance to escape the rarified indignities to come.

"Yes!"

"May I ask if your bottom has ever been taken?" he stopped spanking momentarily.

Hazel didn't reply immediately. Then she finally said, "Yes, but not in the way you're proposing."

"In what way then?"

"I did have a boyfriend who sodomized me."

"I could enjoy doing that myself."

"Oh no, you're too big," she told him, for she had been aware for some time of a jumbo erection pressing against her tummy.

"That's okay, I'd prefer to take you with a nozzle and a hose anyway, at least tonight," he told her, lifting her off his lap. "Get up on the massage table now. And assume a position that renders your bottom accessible."

Hazel stared at him, as though confused by the command. Things were changing quickly! She looked at the massage table.

"Well?" he smacked her on the bottom to encourage her migration across the room.

"Assume a position?" she slowly moved to the table.

"Try getting up on all fours," he suggested while collecting his equipment. Hazel sat on the table. He came over with a fluffy white towel and threw it across the table. "Spread that out first so you won't stick to the leather," he advised. She knelt on the towel and leaned on her hands like a centerfold. He circled her with folded arms. "Drop your chest so that your bottom is uppermost. Bring your knees in a little closer to your chest, and spread your legs even more. Are you comfortable?"

"Uh, sort of," she admitted.

"Hazel, do you know about the word mercy?"

"No."

"Well, that's the word submissives use when they want their dominants to know that some part of the scene isn't going right, or that something hurts too much."

"I understand."

"I see that you can be compliant when you want to be," he ran his fingertips lightly down her back and ended by caressing her curved bottom. "But you haven't been this agreeable all night." He smacked her hard on either cheek. "You behaved disgracefully at The Keep."

"I know."

Robert took the long, slim vibrator out of the Anal Invader box and lubricated it.

'I want you open, Hazel. Every part of you,' he told her, deliberately dividing her labia with deft fingers and lightly probing her slick sex. She squirmed ticklishly as he slipped his middle finger up into her vagina and slowly pistoned it in and out. She arched up to him and opened herself completely.

"You could just fuck me," she suggested suddenly. "You could get up right behind me here and now."

Robert sighed and stopped fingering her.

"I thought you weren't going to try to control this scene," he said.

"I wasn't —"

"Yes you were."

"I just thought that what you were doing just now felt so sexy. And I'm so ready," she appealed timidly.

"Hazel, I'm not saying you didn't have a good idea," Robert told her, coming around in front of her to lightly kiss her and brush her hair away from her face. "But I'm still going to punish you first."

"Okay."

"Now stop trying to seduce me," he ordered, though somehow she was now out of her position and in his arms.

"But you've been hard for such a long time," Hazel softly observed, allowing her hand to brush against his erection. "Don't you need some relief?"

Robert disengaged her arms from around his neck and gently put her back into her original position. "Hazel, behave," he scolded, "you're not in a porno movie."

"I wasn't acting pornographically!" she blushed with embarrassment.

"Yes, you were."

"Isn't a submissive supposed to serve the needs of her dominant?"

"Different dominants have different needs," he explained, firmly separating her knees again to achieve the delicious exposure that shifting her position had lost. "I have a fixation on the female bottom that extends beyond spanking. All I ask is that you allow me to indulge it."

"Oh, certainly!"

"Then be a good girl and stop interrupting me. We've delayed the inevitable long enough."

The next thing Hazel felt was the insertion of the long, cold, slippery vibrator into her bottom. Robert slid it in very slowly. Hazel now forgot all about Robert's cock. All of her attention was immediately focused on herself and what he was doing to her. The anal penetration was almost too much to withstand. His big hands manipulating her ignited a chain of pre-orgasmic winks, the likes of which she had never before experienced. Slipping one hand under her flat belly, he pressed his palm against her abdomen while smacking her filled bottom. Hazel sobbed. If he continued to do things like this she would succumb long before he got to the enema.

Robert took his hand away from her tummy and slid the vibrator out of her bottom, glad he hadn't turned it on.

"You aren't allowed to climax."

"What if I can't help myself?"

"I'll help you," he told her, pressing her down on the table so that she lay flat on her tummy. This was a very good spanking position and he took advantage of it, turning her cheeks pink with his hand. This made not coming even harder. She was as aroused as she had ever been. But so long as he didn't put anything back into her bottom for a while, she knew she could maintain for a few minutes longer.

"Get up on your knees again," he hauled her up by the hips and spread her legs apart. "Now don't move," he warned her and disappeared to fill the hot water bag.

This time Hazel didn't dare move. She knew what was going to happen and was anxious to experience the sensation. Her humiliation was deep, real and profoundly satisfying. He was going to do this. He had thought of it all by himself. It was as though he had read her secret journal, the one that went beyond spanking, just as he had said. Dear, intuitive man. Could they really be so perfectly matched? Robert certainly improved outside the office.

Improvising an IV stand out of a carved wooden coat tree Robert suspended the two-quart enema bag. Then he spread her bottom, lubricated the nozzle and inserted it slowly into her dainty, rose-hued anus.

An ardent bottom worshipper, Robert found his dream in Hazel, for every aspect of bottom was charming, particularly it's sensitivity to pleasure. That Hazel was anally oriented was never more apparent than in her willingness to submit to spanking on that small, tender area. Robert noticed the way her breathing changed while he pushed the nozzle in.

"I love you when you're obedient like this," he told her, gently urging the nozzle in yet a bit farther while pressing his other hand against her flat tummy. Hazel whimpered at this maddening touch, for the palm of his hand was large enough to blanket even the most elusive g-spot. "Hazel, I'm going to start the flow of hot water. Are you ready?"

"How hot is it going to be?"

"Plenty hot."

Hazel couldn't speak for mortification as the water began to fill her. It was very warm, but not unpleasantly so. The nozzle, however, could not but serve the function of a dildo, and felt maddeningly sexy.

"How does that feel?" he asked her suddenly.

"Uh...fine," she replied, a little abashed at how true this was.

"Not too uncomfortable yet?"

"No."

"What are you going to say if something's hurting you?"

"Mercy."

"You're little tummy is becoming quite full," he commented, patting it while twisting the nozzle slightly in her bottom. Hazel felt very warm and almost dizzy by the time the hot water bottle was empty. "Good girl," he told her, slowly removing the nozzle from her bottom. "Don't move," he ordered and left her for a moment in uncertainty. When he returned he showed her a medium-sized rubber anal retention plug. Coating it with the pure, warm juice that bedewed her light brown Venus mound, he then poised it at her anus and attempted to insert it.

"Unclench so I can put this in," he told her.

"I don't dare."

"You're fine."

"What if it pops out?"

"Note the way it tapers then flares, it's designed to stay in. Now open."

Hazel untensed for a fraction of a second. It was long enough for Robert to nudge the tip of the dildo through her anal ring.

"Relax," he ordered, smacking either cheek sharply. She whimpered and relaxed momentarily. He pushed the plug in all the way, patting it firmly into place. "You're doing very well," he complimented her, stroking her tummy and dewy muff. "Are you all right?"

"Yes."

"I hope you haven't forgotten that you have a good paddling coming for playing the trick at the house," he reminded her, physically lifting her off the table, tucking her under one arm and carrying her across to the armless chair. Sitting down and putting her over his lap was the work of a moment.

"Ashamed?" he asked, positioning her properly and pushing the plug in as deeply as it would go.

"Yes," she gasped as he began to spank her on as well as around the plug.

"Uncomfortable yet?" he asked her, reaching under Hazel with one hand to lightly squeeze her tummy. Hazel moaned and twitched across his lap.

"I'm okay," she declared.

"It's remarkable how well you're taking this," he commented before resuming the spanking. "We're going to do this again," he promised. In a few seconds the confluence of sensations caused her to finally climax. Hazel sobbed with emotion as her shuddering subsided and he lifted her off his lap. Without further delay she fled to the commode and locked herself in.

It was a half hour before she joined him in his bedroom. She'd attended to her needs, showered and wrapped herself in a navy cotton robe. Robert had stripped down to green plaid cotton boxers and was lying in his massive bed under the skylight, smoking. He offered her a cigarette but she shook her head with a smile.

"No, I feel too clean."

"Do you feel okay?"

"A little tired."

"Sleepy?"

"Uh-huh."

He put out his cigarette and pulled her against him so that she lay in his arms.

"That was the most fun I ever had with a girl," he admitted freely.

"Even though we didn't even do you-know-what yet?"

"I figure we'll be doing you-know-what in about twenty to forty minutes," he told her, guiding her hand to his on-going erection. "You need a chance to recover first."

"Well, that was the most fun I ever had with a man too," she declared.

"Hazel, I want to do something for you now. Is there anything you want or need? How about that car of yours? Maybe I can get it fixed for you, or let you have a company car to drive."

Hazel pondered the notion of a material reward for a moment or two, then replied, "The best present I could get from you would be permission to write for the magazine the way I originally did, before you forced me to censor and amend the content of my stories."

Robert sat up and looked at her with astonishment. "What are you saying, now?"

"The letters in response to my first issue have come in and they're overwhelmingly positive," she pressed, sitting up on her heels.

"You know, Hazel, my father started Corning in the early sixties and for thirty years employed an all male staff to write confessions in the first person female. When I took over twelve years ago I retired all the old men and hired a female editorial staff. Our sales quadrupled. I think I know what I'm doing."

"Well, what's the good of having an all female staff if you won't listen to their suggestions?" Hazel replied, hurt at the dismissal of her request.

"I suppose the letters have been encouraging," he admitted.

"They don't have editorial restrictions at Augie Rose," she suddenly remembered. "Maybe I'll go and work for them!"

"You'll do nothing of the sort, young lady," he said, taking her across his lap and giving her twelve of the best with the back of a wooden hairbrush through her robe.

"I will if you don't give me back editorial control of my magazine," she stubbornly declared, simultaneously smarting and rushing from the spontaneous paddling.

"Oh, very well, do as you please with the magazine!" he said, lifting her off his lap and scowling blackly. Hazel laughed and cuddled against him. He folded his arms and did not hug her, unable to believe that she had won such an important victory so easily. Hazel pulled back and looked at him.

"You won't be disappointed."

"Well, I suppose I haven't been disappointed in you so far," he unbent a little and even smiled. It was painful giving in, but now that he had done it he felt ready to move on to something more pleasant.

"Oh, and I will take the car," said Hazel gaily.

Chapter Two

Hugo and Bettie

Hugo Sands had all but forgotten that he had a niece until her letter arrived one early Spring day.

"Dear Uncle Hugo," it began, *"You probably don't remember me because the last time you saw me I was only 3. That was 15 years ago, at the last family Christmas dinner you attended.*

It's too bad that you decided to dump the family, because you're the most interesting person in it. My mother has told me repeatedly that you are Satan's avatar. I finally think I understand why.

I must tell you that I have always been into spanking. Ever since I can remember (about age 3 or 4) I have entertained spanking fantasies. The subject of spanking preoccupied me throughout my childhood and once puberty set in, nothing changed.

I've been writing spanking stories for my own amusement since age 8. From ages 11 through 15, I would share them with my girlfriend and we would act them out. We'd pretend they were spy stories, but they always ended in one of us spanking the other one.

Then, I got a boyfriend and stopped playing games with my girlfriend. I initiated spanking foreplay with my boyfriend and received some attention in this area, but he was mostly interested in sex. You know how that goes.

Now I'm about to go to college and boyfriend is about to do the same.

But to get to the point. About a week ago I was in the Combat Zone looking for spanking magazines in an adult bookstore. There was a lot of stuff there, but nothing really pleasant. Then I saw The New Rod

Quarterly. The cover illo was so perfect my heart almost stopped.

I bought the magazine and dismissing my boyfriend, rushed home. The instant I opened to the first page, I was in heaven. The writing was so reflective of what excites me and the illos were just charming. And then there were the letters from people just like me, and those fabulous personal ads. (I already have 3 dates lined up for next week!)

Finally I noticed the masthead: Editor Hugo Sands. I remembered that my mother's maiden name was Sands and that I had an uncle Hugo. My heart went bumpety bump again.

I called my mother to ask her where you lived. She sounded suspicious but told me that she thought you lived out on the Cape. No one I knew had ever heard of or had been to Random Point, so I called information and asked the operator whether it was out on the Cape. She told me that it was.

In September I'll be traveling to California to matriculate at U.C.L.A. If you allow me to visit for the summer, I could work for you writing stories, inputting, doing anything you needed in return for my board. I'd be a model houseguest and never make a mess or play loud music. And I'd be so grateful for the opportunity to get to know my favorite relative better.

> *Sincerely,*
> *Bettie Brandon*

P.S. If you say yes, Mother and I will probably have a big fight over this, but nothing bad will happen. My late father left me a trust fund for college, and I was planning on working away for the summer anyway.

> *B.B."*

Bettie was thoughtful enough to include a photo, which showed her to be a small, slender, olive-skinned sprite with extremely delicate, Mediterranean features and a long mane of tight, glossy, black curls.

Hugo tossed the letter on his desk and lit a cigarette, trying to consider the possible calamities which might arise from granting her wish. In the end he turned to his keyboard and wrote a short, friendly reply, telling her to come whenever she liked.

"Well, I guess it's true that the spanking fetish does run in families," Laura commented that evening as she examined the photo and letter.

"It might run in your family," said Hugo, "but I doubt it does in mine."

"How do you account for this Bettie then?'

"Bettie isn't really a blood relation of mine. Her mother, my sister Louise, was adopted."

"I see," said Laura, not exactly happy to hear this news.

"Don't worry, I'm not going to touch her."

"She's sure to get a crush on you."

"We'll make sure it gets transferred to someone else as soon as possible."

Laura wasn't pleased to be called out of town the eve of Bettie Brandon's arrival. Having submitted a chapter of her graphic novel to a publisher in New York, she was now being summoned to that city to show them the rest. Unwilling to postpone such an important interview, Laura had reluctantly departed from her lover only moments before he drove down to the railroad depot to collect Bettie, who was due on an early evening train.

It was a warm day for early June and Bettie was wearing khaki shorts, hiking boots, sox and a sleeveless, white, cotton halter top that showed a bit of smooth, olive midriff and molded daintily to her small bosom. She was very slender, by no means tall and appeared fragile. The slightness of her frame unsettled Hugo, forcibly reminding him of how young Bettie was.

Bettie had written a fairly spunky letter, but she felt properly timid upon debarking at Random Point. She expected to be met on the platform by a distinguished older gentleman, who was perhaps a bit daffy, in the manner of John Lithgow. Yet the only forty-something male pacing the platform was a tall, sandy haired, custom tailored boomer, sophisticated in the manner of Cary Grant. Deciding that someone this savvy could never be her Uncle Hugo, Bettie walked straight past him, hauling a backpack almost as big as herself.

"Bettie?" the striking man said and she turned in disbelief, almost knocking someone down with her pack.

"Uncle Hugo?"

"Just plain Hugo would be even better," he told her, giving her the perfunctory kiss on the cheek, relieving her of her burden and hoisting it over his own shoulder. The incongruity of the old backpack against his pristine beige suit made her smile. "I can't believe you've been carrying this yourself," he remarked, leading her from the station.

"Oh, I'm deceptively sturdy," she assured him, flexing her calf to reveal a runner's muscle. She was remarkably slim but very well formed, with particularly beautiful skin.

"How did Louise take it when you told her where you were spending the summer?"

"I haven't actually told her. Luckily I have a friend whose family has a cottage in P-town. She's going to let me use it as a return address for Mother all summer."

"Good thinking. But what if she tries to call you?"

"I told her the cottage didn't have a phone."

"Implausible, but original."

"Thank you for letting me come."

"Tell me that after dusting 117 clocks."

"Time must really matter to you!"

"I also own an antiques shop."

"I love old things," she said in a rush, then immediately flushed. Hugo threw the bag in the back of his car and opened the door for Bettie.

On the way home he took her through the village, where he showed her his shop and Marguerite's book store, up the Cliff Road to Anthony Newton's mansion, down again to the beach and then back to his house by the road through the woods.

Bettie stared at him whenever she thought she might risk it. Then they arrived at his old stone house and he took her inside. Bettie was placed in the redecorated attic bedroom, as far away from Laura's room as possible.

"I have a girl friend," Hugo explained as he showed her where everything was. "She's in New York now but she'll be back in a week or so."

"Is she into it?" Bettie asked before wondering whether this was a discreet question.

"She's my illustrator."

"Oh!"

"I'd advise you to turn her into an ally as quickly as possible," Hugo disclosed, piling logs into her hearth for later in the evening. "And by the way," he added, "I'm not really your uncle. Your mother was adopted. I guess she never told you that."

"No, she never did." Bettie sat down on the bench at the foot of the bed and stared at him in astonishment.

"She always knew about it. That's probably why she warned you to stay away from me. She remembered that we aren't blood relations and doesn't trust me with you."

Bettie Brandon was a quiet, intense, thoughtful, cautious, compulsively meticulous little creature that was seen but seldom heard for the first several days of her visit. She wrote constantly in black marble notebooks with cartridge pens and was reading Crime and Punishment. Her favorite walk was to and from the Random Point post office, where Hugo had obtained a box for her to receive correspondence over the summer.

Hugo was disappointed the first time he sat her down at a computer to input some letters, to discover that Bettie couldn't touch type. He shook his head as she began to hunt and peck, knowing that this would never do.

"Young lady, the first thing you're doing is going to summer school to learn how to type," he told her firmly, and the next morning drove her to Woodbridge High School to enroll her in a class. In a couple of days he was gratified to see her attacking the pile of letters without looking at the keyboard.

One afternoon, after presenting Hugo with an almost perfect letters column for his next issue, Bettie said, "Hugo, may I ask your advice?"

"Sure, Bettie, what's on your mind?"

"Well, obviously I've never met someone through an ad before and I'm going on my first date tonight. What should I expect?"

"Who are you seeing?"

"A man named John Philpot. He's coming from Boston. We're meeting at a coffee house in P-town."

"Philpot, eh?" Hugo searched for the name in his customer database. "I can't tell you too much about him, I'm afraid. He's bought three issues of the journal. That's about it. Did you get a photo?"

"No."

"Bad."

"Really?"

"You tell me after the meeting."

"He's 27 and a construction worker. He says he's buff and tanned from his work." Hugo smiled.

"Have you spoken on the phone?"

"No."

"That was your second mistake."

"Why?"

"He might not be your type."

"I never thought to get a phone number," she mused, beginning to feel less than confident about her first scene date.

"You'll know better next time," he told her.

"Do you think he's going to want to, or, I mean, try to ... you know..."

"Spank you?"

Bettie nodded, her flushing rose.

"Well, I'm sure he'll want to, but he probably won't try unless you give him the green light."

"Really?" she brightened. "You mean I don't have to play with him if I don't want to?"

"Of course not."

"But, how do I get out of it if he asks?"

"You mean without hurting his feelings?"

"Yes!"

"I suppose you wrote him a fairly provocative letter?" Bettie nodded with embarrassment. "All right, here's my advice: Plead youth and ignorance. Tell him you've suddenly realized that you're not quite ready to play yet."

"Do you think he'll accept that?"

"He'll be heartbroken but he'll accept it."

"Okay. Good."

"Or, you could be a perfect angel, wear jeans, take a walk down to the coast line and take advantage of a certain fallen drift log that's been in P-town ever since I can remember, and let him give you a dozen or so swats over your pants."

"Really?"

"Why not? You have to get your first spanking sometime and the man's coming all the way from Boston to meet you."

"But, what if I'm not attracted to him?"

"You have a good imagination, close your eyes and pretend he's Val Kilmer."

"Are you serious?" Bettie demanded, thinking, 'I would have said Cary Grant.'

"You know Bettie, spanking is sexy, but it isn't sex. It can be as innocuous as you choose to make it."

"I still want it to be from someone I find very attractive," she said with conviction. "Especially the first time."

"Well, let's hope for the best. But next time, get a photo. Now, how are you getting to P-town?"

"I thought I'd catch a bus."

"Do you have a driver's license?"

"Yes."

"Then you may borrow my car," he told her. Bettie flushed at this mark of favor. Showing up for her date in the bottle green, vintage Jag thrilled her.

Obeying Hugo's suggestion to wear jeans, Bettie departed for Provincetown at seven p.m., more content in the nurturing she was receiving from Hugo than excited by her upcoming date. "If I do let John spank me," thought Bettie, "I'll close my eyes and pretend he's Hugo."

But Bettie returned at nine p.m., unsettled and unspanked. Hugo had just returned from a dinner engagement and was feeding his tomcat baked salmon when Bettie walked in.

"Well, that was fast," he commented.

"I know," she sat down at the wooden kitchen table with a sigh and put her chin on her hand.

"Tell all," Hugo said, filling his wine glass and leaning against the mantle piece to listen.

"You were right," she reported, "He wasn't my type. Worldview a heady mixture of Rush Limbaugh, Howard Stern and Al Bundy. He liked me a lot."

Hugo laughed. "Did you break his heart?"

Bettie hung her head and mumbled, "Yes."

"How did he take it?"

"Oh, he was really nice about it."

"I guess you never walked down to the coast, huh?"

"No. His amphetamine-charged energy scared the hell out of me," she confided.

"You can have a glass of wine if you like," said Hugo. He poured her one and she took a sip.

"Thank you," she said, smiling at him.

"So, who's next on your date list?"

"I have two dates planned for the weekend in Boston and I have a friend I can stay with there."

"Tell me about them."

"One's a young shark in training at the Harvard business school."

"Now that sounds promising," said Hugo, who'd taken his undergrad degree in art history in Cambridge twenty-five years before.

"Who's the other one?"

"Oh. He's an older man," said Bettie, without much enthusiasm.

"How much older?"

"56."

"My god. What ever made you agree to meet him?"

"I don't know," she fretted.

"Do me a favor?" said Hugo, "If I still expect 18 year olds to play with me when I'm 56, get someone to put me out of my misery."

"So, when is your cut-off date for playing with 18 year olds?" she asked shyly.

"About four years ago," he looked at her steadily and said, "and it was inappropriate even then."

Bettie concealed her disappointment in a long sip of wine. "And who was the fortunate 18 year old?"

"My girlfriend's little sister."

"That sounds decadent," Bettie commented, deeply envying this little sister of the terrifying girlfriend she was yet to meet.

"Oh, I was a regular rake in those days, but I've almost totally reformed," Hugo told her.

"I see."

"I know quite a few good players, though, right here in town, without my scruples," he told her. "Just let me know when you run out of personal ad guys to meet and I'll introduce you to them."

Bettie felt hurt that Hugo was so eager to pass her to other men. Then he said, "Do you ever think about getting spanked by other women?"

"No!" she replied violently.

"Just asking."

"I'm sorry, but the idea doesn't appeal to me on any level."

"It's good to know what you want," Hugo approved.

"I didn't mean to snap at you," she apologized.

"That's okay, you've had a stressful day," he sympathized, thinking how easy it would be to take her then and there. "And I know you must be frustrated. That's why I asked you to consider letting Mr. Philpot give you a few swats."

"I want you to do it," she blurted out at great cost to her pride.

"Honey, I would do it in a heartbeat except that's exactly the sort of thing that makes my girlfriend leave me for 6 to 9 months at a time."

"You don't mean to say that you never spank anyone besides your girlfriend?" Now Bettie was surprised. For reading Hugo's editorial's had led her to expect a less conservative attitude.

"Not exactly, but touching you would be dynamite," he explained, in earnest.

"Funny, I'd never think of you as someone who'd be …whipped," she commented recklessly.

After a moment of silence, Hugo smiled faintly and said, "Isn't every man who's in love?"

On the train, which returned Bettie to Random Point the following Sunday afternoon, she recorded the weekend's events in her journal. She gave her first assignation short shrift, eager to describe and analyze Saturday's adventure.

Friday, June 8th

Met first my first older man. Not older like my devastatingly attractive uncle, but really old. Played briefly at his place. Also let him have me. I must be submissive. Make a note: Don't do that again.

The next entry was begun late Saturday night and read as follows:

Saturday June 9th

We met at The Grist Mill on Harvard Square. I walked past the young man with the cell phone and powerbook twice before I finally forced myself to stare at the buttonhole of his suit jacket and acknowledge the pink carnation he had worn for me. My eyes traveled up to the face of Mr. Gilbert Rush, wise guy.

"Ms. Brandon?" Gilbert jumped up the second we made eye contact. He knew who I was. We shook hands, awkwardly on my side, but he smoothed it out like the dealmaker he'd been bred to be.

"What are you reading?" he asked, glancing at my books. "Oh, Dostoyevsky, wonderful! Oh, no, The Fountainhead? Trash!" he dismissed the book that had been giving me wet dreams for the last week with a scornful toss on the table.

"You seem to have strong opinions about literature for a business major," I commented, gathering my books again.

"I got my undergrad degree in English at Princeton," he informed me blithely. "But you can't make any money writing literary criticism, so I went to business school. I just graduated last week."

"Have you made any plans for the future?" I asked, still smarting from the Ayn Rand crack.

"I've been thinking of going out to L.A. and working in my uncle's real estate office for a year or two while I decide what I want to do," he said with a smile.

"Really? Why, I'm going out to L.A. at the end of the summer to start college."

"I remember. U.C.L.A.," he smiled, as if his conquest of me was preordained.

We spent the rest of the time in the restaurant arguing about why I hadn't applied to any Ivy League colleges. I was grilled about my grades, scholarships and loans. At the end of this torture session, during which I think I ate, but didn't taste a thing, he laughed at himself for the absurdity of going out with a child between high school and college. I almost began to hate him.

After dinner we walked over to the gem and stone museum on the campus and toured it for a half hour. I let him do most of the talking. He lectures like an academic. It's a shame he's only going to become a businessman.

Next we took a walk around the campus. He seemed to be trying to decide what to do with me. Finally he invited me back to his studio apartment. It was located on the top floor of a 100-year-old walk-up in Cambridge with a wonderful skyline of connecting rooftops and a patch of Harvard green in the near distance. The big room had bay windows overlooking the busy, narrow street and letting in the noise of the jazz coffeehouse below.

One glance at the interior and I knew that Mr. Rush came from wealth. There wasn't a wooden electrical spool table or cinderblock bookcase in sight. But there was enough Ralph Lauren linen to go around and this man's stereo system needed its own suite of furniture.

The second he walked in he began to listen to messages, read faxes and return calls. He had to turn on his computers, check his E-mail and completely change his clothes before he felt comfortable enough to relax on the sofa with me. Neurofreak.

On the positive side, he personally ground our coffee, which he served to me in pretty china and I couldn't help but notice not one but two fresh, florist-perfect bouquets decorating his mantelpiece and coffee table. He cared.

Once he had me in arm's reach he began to complain about how small I am. He said I have no bottom. I protested and allowed him to turn me over his knee and examine the area closely.

Once I was over and under his hand he felt how round my bottom is. Then he complimented me and pulled my skirt up to examine my panties. He claimed he liked my plain cotton Calvins, but then did nothing but complain about them, telling me how much he liked frills. (Maybe he's a latent homosexual. He's goddamned fussy enough. This guy really does belong in L.A.!)

Finally he started to spank me (!!!) over my panties. It was a little too hard at first and I told him so. He scowled that I was a baby, but went lighter. That made all the difference and I began to really get into my first spanking. Oh, and for all his arrogance and foolishness, what a fine spanker he is! What flutters I felt! It was divine.

Pretty soon he pulled my panties down and all the way off and began all over again on the bare. I don't know how long he spanked me, but I didn't want him to stop. When he did, it was to pull off the rest of my clothes and make love to me. That part was very good too. Except it didn't last quite long enough.

After making love he reverted to the same superior attitude that had overshadowed our first conversation, making several remarks about my youth and inexperience that cast me in the light of a pesky kid. Naturally I felt upset when he began to check his answering machine, (which had been mercifully turned down for 35 minutes) within three minutes of having an orgasm.

At least he got to have an orgasm. I didn't have time to and he didn't inquire. Feeling somewhat deflated I got dressed and headed for the door.

"Wait a minute, where do you think you're going, young lady?" he looked up from his phone to ask.

"You look busy," I mumbled, eager to flee. Suddenly I didn't feel completely welcome.

"You'll go when I tell you to. Sit down," he told me firmly and got off the phone in a moment. "Now, what's going on?"

"I thought I'd better go and wait for the train back to Random Point."

"Random Point, is that where you're from?"

"I'm staying there for the summer with my uncle, Hugo Sands," I said, knowing that dropping the name would change a good deal and not liking him for that. In fact, except for being a sublime spanker and an okay stud, Mr. Rush is a real bore.

"Is that so? Well, I see you're very well connected," he commented, predictably. "Perhaps I'll drive you home myself. I'd love to meet your uncle."

"I don't think he'd like that," I lied.

"And why not?" he demanded, "I should think an uncle would be deeply concerned about who was seeing his niece."

"I promised I would never bring a guest home without permission. Surely you don't want me to incur my uncle's wrath?"

"He spanks you quite often, doesn't he?" Gilbert dropped his affected air of self-importance momentarily to indulge in a fantasy.

"He hasn't done it once yet."

"I find that rather hard to believe, my delectable one," he said, throwing a few things into a leather portfolio and ushering me out.

At first it seemed as though he was going to drive me back to Random Point and try to meet Hugo anyway. But on the way out of the city I happened to mention to Gilbert what I'd done the night before with the older man.

Gilbert didn't take it well. I won't say that he yelled at me, because he's not the type to raise his voice, but he scolded me as though he had a right to, taking the sort of tone I'd expect from an avowed lover, but no one else. He couldn't believe that I had let a man have me just because I felt sorry for him. He said it showed the weakness of resolve and overall immaturity one had to expect in an 18 year old, yet grievously lamented my lapse, as though it had somehow lessened the purity of our encounter, for he'd been pleased to assume that he had been the first man to spank me. He was the first cute man. But I decided not to give him the satisfaction of bringing this up!

I stopped him, making him turn the car around and take me back to the train station! He had made me so angry that I could barely speak, but I finally stammered out what I thought of him. I said that I was not "Tess of The D'Urbervilles" to be excoriated for a moral transgression by some soulless real estate developer with a cell phone permanently welded to his braincase. Then I said, "Let me out!"

Gilbert parked and stayed with me till the train came, trying to reason with me.

"Look, sweetheart, you're just over-excited. It's been a big day," he soothed me, patting my hand as we sat on the bench. I gave him a look and he backed off.

"You make me sick," I told him boldly. Then I turned my back on him and opened The Fountainhead.

He sat and looked at me, trying to think of how to rescue whatever esteem I'd had for him earlier on. I was gratified to see him looking crestfallen as the train pulled out. But catching me looking at him through the window changed his frown to a bright smile. It is a very nice smile. Too bad it belongs to a ridiculous man!

On Monday Bettie received an express mail letter from Gilbert that read:

Dear Bettie,
That was a pretty good telling off you gave me. But it actually made me think better of you. Dearest and most beautiful girl, since we are both going to be in California pretty soon, don't you think we should give this another chance?
   Love, Gilbert
P.S. I'm determined to visit you in Random Point and meet your uncle Hugo and will write to him this moment for an appointment.
   G.

As soon as Bettie opened her letter she rushed over to the shop to find Hugo in his office going through his mail.

"Hugo, please see if there's a letter from Gilbert Rush," she asked imperatively. Hugo leafed through the large pile and came up with a letter on heavy cream vellum stationary embossed with Gilbert's name and address in burgundy.

"Gilbert Rush?"

"The boy I met over the weekend."

"Really? Why is he writing to me?"

"He wants to meet you."

"Before I read this, tell me what happened," said Hugo with interest. So Bettie described her date.

"Okay, now I'll read the letter," said Hugo, quite delighted that his little publication had already enabled his charming relation to enjoy several adventures.

Dear Mr. Sands,

I had the privilege over the weekend of meeting your niece, Bettie and naturally she knocked me off my feet. I would like the opportunity of paying my formal addresses to her this summer while she resides in Random Point. Bettie has told me that permission had to be arranged through you before she could receive visitors at your home and I am therefore writing to you to apply for it.

My intentions are strictly honorable and to this end I will ask you now to pull my personal ad from all future issues of your wonderful publication. It has enabled me to meet several charming young ladies over the past year and has been my only hope for eventually finding a life partner. I think I've found her, if she'll have me.

Fortuitously, I had planned to move to California in the fall to pursue a career in real estate in my uncle's firm. This should coincide perfectly with Bettie's matriculation at U.C.L.A. I will help her get excellent grades.

I hope to be in Random Point on Friday evening and if it is convenient for you, I look forward to meeting you then.

> *Sincerely,*
> *Gilbert Rush*

"Well, I'll say one thing," Hugo observed, "he's focused."

"May I see?" she asked, with a pounding heart. Hugo handed her Gilbert's letter and she flushed a deep rose while reading it. "Oh! Of all the nerve," she commented. "He's taking a lot for granted here!"

"He's asked me to pull his ad," Hugo reminded her. And indeed, that one portion of the letter pleased her. But the bulk seemed pretentious, condescending and patently absurd.

"Pay his addresses?" she asked.

"Tiger goes a courtin'," Hugo noted.

"As though I'd want my life partner to be some predatory businessman!" she declared scornfully.

"Bettie, what was it exactly that you had the fight about?" Hugo asked, giving her the letter to keep. She sighed and told Hugo about her adventure with the older man. Hugo concealed his indignation at her misdirected generosity masterfully, smoking a cigarette while she told the story and reminding himself that Gilbert had already said a good deal to Bettie on the subject.

"I'm just curious about one thing, Bettie. Why did you let the older man spank you and not the construction worker? You told me you only wanted to play with someone you found attractive."

"I think it was because Mr. Philpot scared me. I thought, once this guy starts, he's not going to want to stop and I won't be able to control him. Whereas the older man was both less tentative and less threatening. So I just went along with the program. Was that wrong, Hugo?"

"It's never wrong to do an act of kindness," Hugo said encouragingly. "But I do think that sticking to your original plan of only playing with people you're attracted to will be better for your head in the long run."

"Oh, I intend to," said Bettie, relieved to avoid a second scolding for her hapless promiscuity.

"However, I can perfectly understand Gilbert's amazement and concern at your doing such a thing," Hugo said decisively.

"Really? You think he had a right to talk to me like that?"

"Bettie?"

"Yes?"

"I think we're going to let Mr. Rush visit, don't you?"

The week passed without any further communication between Bettie and Gilbert. Meanwhile Hugo had politely called Gilbert with his address and consent to the visit on Friday.

On the morning of that day Hugo said to Bettie, "I expect your suitor will be showing up between four and seven, so don't wander too far away this afternoon."

"This is ridiculous," she muttered, vehemently cracking a soft-boiled egg. "I don't even like him!"

Hugo smiled and returned to his paper. "Not even a little?"

"Just for sex, maybe," she replied thoughtfully.

"Tell him that and see how he takes it," Hugo chuckled.

"I will," she promised.

Gilbert arrived, as Hugo predicted, at four p.m., driving a small, new Mercedes convertible. The cut of his suit impressed even Hugo and he carried orchids for Bettie.

Bettie appeared in a white halter dress and ankle lacing espadrilles. She didn't speak more than two sentences as she served them tea in Hugo's drawing room while the men spoke of Harvard, then and now. This was an unanticipated bond that disturbed Bettie. Gilbert's manner was friendly but deferential, as became his age and position in life. Bettie was neither discussed nor addressed.

When Gilbert found out about Hugo's antiques shop in the village he insisted on purchasing a present for his mother. All three of them went to the shop where Gilbert asked Hugo to make a suggestion. Remembering the make of Gilbert's car, Hugo suggested an expensive cherry wood vanity set. Gilbert handed over a credit card without concern, telling Bettie how pleased his mother would be. Bettie was mortified, feeling as though more was being bought and sold here than a vanity.

Less than an hour had passed since Hugo and Gilbert had first shaken hands when Hugo suddenly looked at his watch and pleading a prior engagement, abandoned his niece to her admirer.

"Well!" Gilbert breathed, his face wreathed in smiles.

"You're despicable," she told him curtly and began walking home.

"Pardon me?"

"I can't believe you were showing off to my uncle like that!"

"Showing off?" Gilbert seemed perplexed.

"Pretending you had to buy your mother a present and spending so much money in the shop. That was just to buy Hugo's good will. Admit it!" she angrily demanded.

"Why shouldn't I admit it? It's in my best interest to gain your uncle's good will. I happen to think he has influence with you."

"Well, he doesn't. In fact seeing how easily he was taken in by you has greatly reduced my respect for Hugo Sands."

"He wasn't taken in by me. He understands my motives better than I do myself. And furthermore, I'm sure he approves of them."

"You really do take a lot for granted."

"Where are we going?"

"I don't know," she said unhelpfully.

"How about coming back to the inn where I'm staying and having dinner with me there?"

"I suppose it would do no harm," she reluctantly agreed. They then proceeded to the 150-year-old Bone and Feather Inn, where Gilbert had rented the Magistrate's Suite.

"Bettie, I realize I made a poor impression on you last week, but believe me, I'm not the Victorian you accused me of being. I simply recoiled at the thought of your pearly perfection being pawed by a hoary old hand. I wasn't jealous, just revolted," Gilbert explained.

"Thank you for clarifying that," she said politely. "I feel better now." They entered the Bone and Feather Pub and sat in a red leather booth. Connie brought Gilbert a wine list and didn't bother to card Bettie. Gilbert put his chin on his hand and stared at her.

"Why are you looking at me?" she asked, with mounting color.

"Does it upset you to be admired?"

"You only admire me now because my uncle is someone important. Before you knew about Hugo, I was just an annoying kid that you allotted exactly 35 minutes of your sexual energy to and never expected to see again."

"Bettie, how can you say such things?" Gilbert seemed shocked.

"By the way, where's your cell phone today?"

"I know how much you hate it, so I left it home."

Bettie regarded him with skepticism. "You couldn't live for twenty minutes without banging on some kind of keyboard," she accused.

"You don't know how wrong you are," he smiled. "If you were to come up to my room, for instance, you'd be hard put to find a single telecommunications device."

She smiled faintly but did not commit. They spent the rest of the meal discussing literature and he determined that in spite of Ayn Rand, she had elegant taste for a high school girl, worshipping Aldous Huxley, Oscar Wilde, and Colette. It disquieted Gilbert that her beauty had distracted him from noticing her intellect the previous week. He was supposed to notice everything. Nonetheless, at the end of their meal, she agreed to come up to his room.

"I want you to come visit me in Boston next weekend," he said, making her sit next to him on the loveseat facing the hearth. "Will you?"

"Ask me tomorrow," she told him.

"I must say, Bettie, you aren't being very nice today," Gilbert observed, becoming impatient with her aloofness.

"You weren't very nice to me last week."

"If I scolded you it was only for your own good. You can't go around giving in to every man who tells you he's a dominant. It isn't sensible or healthy."

"I'll give in to anyone I please," she declared, folding her arms across her pert bosom.

"Not if I have anything to say about it you won't," he returned, with equal stubbornness.

"Well, you don't"

"I certainly will," he told her, removing his jacket and unknotting his tie.

"I'm a free spirit," she said with conviction.

"You're a spoiled brat!" he told her, rolling up his sleeves.

The next thing she knew he had taken her over his knee. He commenced spanking her heart-shaped bottom through her summer dress, gripping her firmly by her tiny waist as he brought his palm down smartly on either cheek several dozen times.

When he pulled up her skirt she didn't protest. Her clinging white briefs were of fine Calais lace, allowing her smooth olive skin to show through its filigree.

"I see you took my advice and went lingerie shopping," he approved, patting her small but perfectly rounded seat affectionately. Bettie bit her lip to prevent herself from telling him off while in this position. In a moment he began to spank her again and spent the next several minutes thoroughly warming the seat of her panties. Meanwhile Bettie floated on a wave of indescribable sensation.

"Free spirit, indeed," he said, finally pulling her panties down, to reveal a bottom already blushing dark rose from his hand "You're just a bad little girl who needs a good spanking!"

"No!" she protested, reaching back to rub her bottom for the first time.

"Don't tell me no," he snapped, taking her by the wrist and slapping her on the back of her hand. "Ow!" she cried, and put her hand back in front of her. "I'm going to teach you better manners," he promised.

"Your manners aren't anything to brag about, you know," she pointed out, hoping he would pause to rub her bottom. Her accusation interested him.

"And what's wrong with my manners?" he demanded.

"You completed our first sex act without so much as asking me whether I had climaxed," she reminded him, "and were checking your answering machine within seconds of withdrawal!"

This declaration stayed Gilbert's hand in mid-swat. "What's this you're saying now? I didn't get you off?" he turned her around on his lap to look at her face. "Then what was all that whimpering about?"

"Those are just the sounds I make during sex. I don't make any sound when I come. I just breathe harder. You'll see what I mean if it ever happens."

"What do you mean, if? You tell me what it takes to get you off and I'll do it."

"I'm not going to tell you. You'll have to find out for yourself through trial and error."

"Goody. Let's start with caning and an anal plug!" Gilbert put her off his lap and went to fetch the small cane he'd brought with him.

"Hey, I'm not ready for caning!" she protested. "That hurts too much." But she said nothing against the other suggestion, though it made her blush more deeply.

"Oh, don't be such a baby," he chided her, flexing the cane and slapping it against one hand. "You're not afraid of me, are you?"

"Not of you so much as the cane."

"Don't you think you've earned six of the best with your fresh remarks?"

"No way in hell."

"Well, I do. Bend over."

"I will not!" she folded her arms stubbornly.

"Look, I've caned women before. I know what I'm doing. I promise I won't cane you any harder than I would a 12 year old."

"You'd cane a twelve year old?"

"Of course not," he patiently replied, "I meant that by way of example."

"Oh."

"Now come on," he said, taking her by the hand and making her bend over with her hands on the seat of a straight-backed chair. She didn't resist the placement and was aware of her heart contracting with excitement as he handled her. She looked back at him over one shoulder with large, solemn brown eyes. This made him lean down and kiss her. "That's better," he said. "You know I'll take good care of you."

Bettie knew nothing of the sort but was beginning to grow accustomed to Gilbert's abrupt ways. Then she had a thought that made her smile. Gilbert seemed to know more about spanking women than he did about making love to them.

"What's amused you?" he demanded, noticing her expression.

"Nothing."

"I'll get it out of you," he promised, laying the cane against her skirt and tapping her with it once before taking careful aim and delivering the first lightly stinging stroke across the center of her seat. Since this was no more than a sharp tap, Bettie gave a little wriggle and waited. The next stroke, placed just below the first, was more like an actual cane stroke and surprised a gasp out of Bettie. She felt one sharp pang, and then the echo of it as it penetrated under her skin, even through her skirt and panties, which she'd pulled back up. Gilbert paused and let the sting fade, stroking Bettie's bottom through the skirt. Bettie thought, "That kind of hurt, but it was sexy too!"

"Bettie?"

"Yes?"

"Answer, 'Yes, Sir,' when I have you in this position," he recommended, tapping her lightly with the cane.

"Yes, Sir!" she immediately replied, in dread of the damage even one harsh cane stroke might do.

"Do you know why you're being disciplined?"

"No, Sir," she said, shivering as he pulled up her skirt and gathered it at her waist. Bettie kept her feet together and her legs straight, wishing she'd worn sexier shoes.

"You're being punished for being a rude little girl."

"How am I rude?"

"Here it's been a whole week since we were together and you haven't even told me that you're happy to see me." Gilbert punctuated this complaint with the second real cane stroke, placed across the plumpest portion of her bottom. This stroke made her jump, cry out and reach back to rub her bottom at once. She whimpered indignantly as the sting penetrated for a second or two. Yet his sternness caused a flutter in her tummy that kept returning throughout the remainder of the caning.

"I guess I was offended by the way you spoke to me," she said at last.

"I simply scolded you. Get used to it," he told her coolly, administering another juicy cut, just above the last one.

"Ow!" she cried and broke her position to stand up and rub.

"That was three," he told her, gently pushing her back down. "Do you think you could manage to hold still for the next three?"

"Not if they're going to be that hard!" she cried.

"I'll compromise with you," Gilbert said magnanimously, "I'll lighten my stroke if you agree to take the next three on the bare bottom."

"I agree," she said at once.

Gilbert pulled her panties down and helped her step out of them. "Spread your legs and let me see you," he told her, pressing his palm between her thighs and feeling the dew on her sable Venus mound. While he had her in this position he divided her cheeks to examine her intimately. Bettie's tiny clitoris began to throb painfully in response to this attention, especially when Gilbert slipped one long, middle finger in between the petals of her damp, little pussy. "That's a good girl," he told her, pulling out his finger, dripping wet. "Don't move," he told her, leaving her momentarily to dig into his suitcase for a slim, 6" vibrator and a bottle of Astroglide he'd picked up at the drugstore in Boston.

"What's that?" she turned her head in surprise.

"Eyes front," he told her firmly. "It's just something to help you take the rest of your caning like the adorable little girl that you are. Now come over here," he said, taking her by the forearm and pulling her over to the canopied four-poster.

He piled two pillows on top of each other at the edge of the bed and bent her over them, which lifted her feet off the floor. Sitting beside her, he pushed her thighs as far apart as they would go and spread her bottom cheeks. Suddenly, to her mingled shame and pleasure, she felt a few drops of the cool, slippery lubricant fall upon her exposed anus. "Hold still," he warned her firmly, grasping the pharmacy dildo and positioning the rounded end against her rosy, bottom hole. "Relax," he urged her, spreading her open with his hands and nudging the tip of the vibrator in an inch. As he began this process Bettie started to whimper and wriggle, not exactly trying to get away, but not exactly helping him either. "Didn't I tell you to hold still?" he demanded, slapping her smartly on either cheek. "And stop clenching. This is going in," he told her, pushing the dildo in another inch. She groaned and gave her tail a little shake, as though to expel it, earning her six hard swats that left their rose imprint on either cheek.

This treatment caused a series of conflicting emotions in Bettie's tender bosom, beginning with mortification but blending into ticklish excitement. Her clit against the pillow throbbed severely and her own pearly essence bedewed her smooth thighs.

"You pretend to be so grown-up," he gently teased her, pushing the dildo in deeper, then massaging her bottom around it, "but that's not what you fantasize about." He tapped the toy in deeper. "I went back and read your first letter."

"Oh!"

"Oh, indeed. There was one sentence that fascinated me. It read, and I quote: 'I am anal-erotic but have never been forced to confront this facet of my sexuality.' What an interesting choice of words, Bettie, why forced?"

"It seems sexier that way," she admitted.

"And how would you feel if I forced you to have a climax with this vibrator in your bottom?"

"I...would be... most grateful," she replied.

"That may happen presently, but meanwhile, we still have to finish your caning," he decided, burying the dildo so deeply between her smooth buttocks that only an inch protruded.

Bettie marveled at how great a distraction the vibrator was. She seemed to hardly feel the sting of the remaining cane strokes and was almost sorry to see him lay it aside. Picking up a light, maple hairbrush, Gilbert sat on the edge of the bed, took her back across his knee and spanked her soundly.

Bettie lay across his knee as meekly as a child, but throbbed with womanly passion as sensation succeeded sensation. Her pussy was perfectly placed against his trousered lap to grind and the invasive toy was driving her nearly mad with excitement. As he smacked her with the hairbrush she rose to meet the strokes, but he liked her better flat against his lap and pressed her down with a hand on her waist.

Abruptly he put the hairbrush down and soothed her with his hand. Then he began to lightly twist and rotate the dildo in her bottom. Bettie sobbed with humiliation and had never felt more aroused. Finally he twisted the end and turned on the little vibrator. He had not administered eight more spanks to his beautiful captive when an unmistakable spasm rippled through her lithe little frame and she then collapsed, limp and panting across his lap.

Extracting the vibrator was the work of a moment. Then Gilbert turned her around and took her in his arms. She shuddered against him, with her face hidden in his lapel, feeling unbearably shy.

"Well?" he asked, making her look at him.

"Well, what?" she tried to wriggle off his lap.

"Tell me that you love me," he demanded.

"I love you," she replied, with a reluctant smile.

"But not unreservedly," he brooded, pushing her off his lap. "What more do I have to do to prove worthy of your affection?"

"Not patronize me."

"Impossible, seeing as you're a silly child and I'm a responsible adult."

"What's so responsible about you?"

"I can afford to take a vacation this summer, but I'd rather put in 40 hours a week at an investment banking firm in order to get some practical experience."

"Great, you're only 23 and already you're a workaholic," she declared, unimpressed.

"I am not a workaholic," he said firmly, "but I am a go-getter. Some day you'll be glad of that, young lady."

Bettie suddenly realized how serious his intentions were.

"Oh, you'll forget all about me once those sleek, Beverly Hills playgirls check you out," said Bettie, imagining shrewd, tanned husband hunters swarming down the strip in pink convertibles.

"We'll see about that," he promised confidently, not seeing how he could possibly do better than the exquisite niece of the best-connected gentleman in the scene.

"So tell me the truth, Elizabeth," said Gilbert to Bettie as they walked in the woods the next morning, "does Hugo spank you or doesn't he?"

It was a balmy day with soft, perfumed air and a deep blue sky. The previous night was the first that Bettie had ever spent alone with a man and she was feeling very grown up. She had even forgotten to call Hugo and tell him she would not be home that night. Somehow, he had figured it out and did not seem at all surprised to see her return at ten a.m. only to change her clothes, as Gilbert was waiting outside.

"I wish he did. I find him very attractive," Bettie confessed. "But so far he has adopted a strict hands-off policy."

"I wonder why," Gilbert mused, mystified. "You know I've been getting your uncle's publications for about 5 years and I've always thought of him as some kind of spanking Svengali. I can't believe he's been able to resist an enchanting and compliant 18-year-old right under his roof. That's like finding out that Hunter S. Thompson doesn't smoke dope."

"It astonished me too, but there's a simple explanation. He's in love with the young lady who does the illustrations for his magazine and apparently this love has domesticated him."

"I wouldn't let Hugo hear you put it that way," Gilbert chuckled, pulling her into a sun-dappled copse.

"But even though he hasn't spanked me, he has given me the benefit of his advice."

"Oh? And what was his advice with regard to me?"

"Give me a break, you know damn well you're in the Good Old Boy Club. He's practically wrapped me up in ribbon for you."

Gilbert smiled. "No," she continued, "he's told me important things."

"Like what?"

"Like how to answer letters."

"You mean letters from the personal ads?" He tried to take her down to the grass but she tugged him by the hand a little further into the woods. Finally they came to the brook. Now they selected a smooth, flat rock and sat down side by side.

"I love the brook," she sighed, hugging her knees to her chest in her flattering blue jeans shorts and red and white gingham halter-top. Ankle high hiking boots and thick sox completed the outfit and she had her very long, tightly rippling hair partially clipped back. Her slender, well-turned legs with their distinctive olive tone mesmerized him with their shiny smoothness and he ran one hand up her shin.

"What kind of letters?" Gilbert persisted. "You aren't still answering personal ads, are you, Elizabeth?" Bettie's heart jumped at his tone.

"Not so far. But I may do so in the future. After all, in a few months I'll be able to answer California ads."

"Now just a minute, didn't we just establish that you love me?"

"Oh! You meant love in that sense?"

"What did you think I meant, darling?"

"I thought you meant love your ability to make me climax," she replied guilelessly.

"Oh," he said, taken aback and going over the conversation in his mind again to check for meaning. "Well, be that as it may, for now, let's return to the subject of your answering ads. Surely Hugo showed you my letter and you know that I've pulled my own ad."

"Yes, I have that letter," Bettie said.

"I've pulled my ad because of you."

"I didn't tell you to do that," Bettie said in a tone that made him want to shake her. Gilbert took a deep breath and marshaled his annoyance. Hugo must have been counseling her rigorously, Gilbert mused, for he had never encountered a girl of her age with quite so much poise. He had envisioned a far different slant to their relationship, which she now appeared to be running.

"I did it as an investment in our future, dear," said Gilbert pleasantly, kissing her hand. "You don't really want me to date other women, do you?"

"This is all so sudden."

"Oh, it is not!" he cried with exasperation. "You've had a week to mull my letter over. What did you think I was saying if not that I want you to be my girlfriend?"

"But just last week you were saying how silly it would be to date a girl of my age."

"It would be silly if she were an average girl, but you aren't. If anything, you're a bit too sophisticated for your age," he reflected.

"There's only one thing wrong with your scenario," said Bettie.

"And that is?"

"I find it difficult to relate to businessmen. I was hoping for an artist or writer."

"How many artists do you know who are making a living?"

"I don't intend to rely on a man to support me," Bettie asserted.

"Why not? Then you could be the artist or writer and it wouldn't matter if you made any money or not."

"I see you don't have much confidence in my earning ability."

"I just want to provide for you myself."

Bettie suddenly melted and put her arms around his waist. "Aren't you sweet," she murmured, laying her head against his chest.

"I'm glad you finally noticed," he said, locking his arms around her. "Now promise you won't answer any more ads."

"No." She pulled away and flashed him a stubborn look.

"Why not?"

"I want to have adventures."

"Like you had last Friday night?"

"No. But maybe with a professor or two."

"Bettie, that never works," he began to counsel her patiently, then noticed that her eyes looked quite mischievous and that she was laughing at him. "You're teasing me, aren't you?"

"I don't know. Am I?"

"Let's find out," he said, reaching for her waist to pull her across his lap. She didn't resist and allowed him to position her perfectly. "What a horrible little girl you are!" he declared, bringing his hand down hard on the seat of her jeans shorts.

"But how can I resist the temptation of being spanked by other men?" she provoked him. Five or six smacks communicated his frustration.

"Guess what, you're not going to find a more compatible playmate than me if you look all 4 years of college." Smack! Smack! Smack!

"But I won't know that until I start experimenting," she maintained, really liking the feel of his hard hand through the denim shorts. The kind of heat produced by these attentions was not unpleasant and her tiny clitoris throbbed to life. His palm came down relentlessly on either cheek as he gave her a long, hard spanking by the edge of the stream. Towards the end she was ready to admit that it would not be easy to do better than Gilbert for the sort of titillation she craved.

When he finally let her up she could trace the impressive outline of his cock under his smooth, khaki trousers. "There! See what you've done?" he accused, taking her in his arms to kiss her.

Gilbert had no conception of the temptations confronting Bettie that summer as Hugo assigned her the task of inputting the personal ads for his magazine on a daily basis. In less than two weeks in Random Point, Bettie went from a total novice to a cynical and experienced connoisseur of attitude and technique in the dominant male. Having Hugo to advise her had done little to preserve her innocence.

On the evening of Laura Random's return, Gilbert also called to visit and spirit Bettie away to a weekend in Vermont. Thus Laura met Bettie and her lover at the same time and could not fail to be charmed at what a handsome couple they made.

"See? I told you I'd find a distraction for Bettie," Hugo told Laura as they watched Gilbert put Bettie in his car and drive away.

"And nothing happened between you two all this time?"

"She's been too busy to even give me a thought," Hugo assured the skeptical Laura.

"What an attractive young man. I wish I could get him to pose for me," said Laura.

"I'm sure that all you'd have to do is ask."

"Do you think that Bettie would mind?"

"I think it would be just the thing to make her appreciate what she's got."

As Laura predicted, Bettie did not approve of Gilbert posing for her, though she said nothing at all when the interchange took place before her when they returned from the weekend in Vermont. Gilbert was overwhelmed by this attention from the beautiful Laura Random and immediately agreed.

"I draw from photos. May I take your picture next time you're in Random Point?"

"That will be next week," he said happily. "What should I wear?"

Bettie was unaware that she was brooding while Gilbert and Laura discussed outfits. After Gilbert departed for Boston, Hugo said, "I'm sure you'll want to photograph Bettie too."

"You read my mind," said Laura, "I was just thinking of costumes to put this little goddess in."

"Me?"

"I could create a new character with you as the model," said Laura, pulling Bettie by the hand up to her room. "Have you ever been fitted for a corset?"

Hugo breathed a sigh of relief. There was nothing like an in-depth corsetry discussion to promote female bonding. Besides, he had observed Bettie's fine lips curve into a smile when Laura flattered her. All and all, Hugo was pleased with the adventure of being an uncle. And the timely addition of Gilbert to their summer added the balance necessary to true domestic felicity.

However, this did not stop Bettie from continuing to covet Hugo in her heart. As the summer neared an end she became oppressed by the thought of departing from Hugo without having ever gotten closer to him that she was on the first day of her arrival.

Indeed, it was the day before her departure for California when her frustration reached a fever pitch and she decided to confront Hugo with her request for the second time.

"So you want some attention, do you?" Hugo did not look displeased this time. "Well, you're in luck, because I've arranged a really special going-away party for you tonight."

"A party? For me?"

"I think it's time you were initiated into our little group."

"Initiated?"

"You did say you wanted a spanking."

"But...in public? I mean, in front of other people?"

"Don't worry, they'll all be friends. You've worked hard all summer and behaved yourself nicely. You deserve a night of decadence. In the best of taste, of course."

Bettie flushed all over, thinking of the various men she had met in the course of the summer in Random Point and wondering whether they'd be at the party. There was that tall, blond and handsome Detective Flagg, whom she had talked out of giving her a speeding ticket in July. There was the blade-like architect, William Random, to whom Hugo had her deliver a music box for his sweetheart. There was Anthony Newton, the musical composer. Hugo had sent Bettie to him several times to type letters. Would all of these men and their sophisticated female companions attend at her party, Bettie wondered? And what did one wear?

"Someone has to be the first to spank Bettie," Hugo said to

Marguerite confidentially that evening, "why not Malcolm?"

"Oh, Hugo, I think he feels self-conscious playing in a situation like this. He never has, you know," Marguerite explained, sipping liberally from her champagne glass.

"Can you think of a better time for him to come out than initiating an eighteen year old girl at her first party?"

"It would certainly give him a great deal of face," Marguerite mused, "I'll go and propose it to him."

"Good girl. And once he's engaged, maybe you and I can have some fun, for old time's sake."

"Okay, Hugo," Marguerite fairly sparkled at her ex-patron who continued to hold a place of importance in her heart.

Marguerite found Malcolm deeply engaged in conversation with William Random on the subject of sub-zero sleeping bags.

"Darling, Bettie has to get a spanking sooner or later, why don't you go and do it?" the snugly gowned redhead suggested, as though she were asking him to refill the ice cube trays.

"Excuse me?" Malcolm stared at his wife in amazement.

"Malcolm, I told you that this party was Bettie's farewell. Tomorrow she's going off to California and we won't see her again until Christmas at least. Make her feel loved before she leaves us."

"But, I've never even talked to the girl," he protested, flushing with embarrassment at the thought of laying hands on the exquisite little Bettie in front of everyone.

"Forget the formalities," his wife advised.

"What am I supposed to do, now?" Malcolm eyed Bettie narrowly across the room, which she had just entered with Susan Ross.

"Just go up to her and say, 'Bettie, my name is Malcolm. We've met in the village a few times. Do you remember me? Oh, splendid. Well, would you like to play?'"

"And then what do I do with her?"

"Ask her if she wants to play here or in private."

"And where do I take her?"

"Just go upstairs. One of the bedrooms should do nicely. William, wait 25 minutes, then relieve him," Marguerite instructed confidently. "She's been reading The Fountainhead and envisioning you in a quarry all summer."

"What if she doesn't want to play with me?" Malcolm was skeptical that such a direct approach could work between almost total strangers, though the more he looked at Bettie, the more interested he became in testing the plan.

Forgetting all but the substance of his lines, Malcolm stepped up to Bettie, and bluntly blurted out, "Bettie, would you consent to let me spank you?"

Bettie stared at Malcolm with a quickening pulse and nodded, taking him by the hand and lithely leading him out of the room. Malcolm followed her crisscross-backed beige and white checked sundress up two pair of stairs to the attic studio where she had spent the happiest summer of her life.

They talked for a few minutes, Bettie sharing her hopes and literary dreams with the successful young chain bookstore owner. Then she spoke of how meeting her uncle Hugo had changed her life and even mentioned the impossible young man whom she had met through a personal ad in her uncle's publication.

Malcolm admitted that he had found his Marguerite through a similar personal ad and reluctantly acknowledged that he owed his present happiness in part to Hugo Sands. He did not, of course, add how much he resented and distrusted Hugo Sands for the inordinate influence he still seemed to exert over his wife.

Then suddenly there seemed to be nothing more to say and Malcolm adjusted his buttoned down mind to the concept of pure sensation.

At length Malcolm soberly told Bettie that it was time for her spanking. She came to him wide-eyed as he sat on the low, oaken bed and took her across his lap. Bettie had never been spanked in her own bedroom by an older man (he was 31) and felt quite overwhelmed by the young daddy aspect he projected.

He pulled up her skirt and rolled her panties down to mid-thigh to expose her bottom completely. Then he spent some minutes caressing and massaging her, until she was so relaxed that her smooth thighs spread voluntarily, and he was able to inhale her budding scent. He began to spank her firmly, though not severely. His big hand nearly covered her whole bottom. But she had taken quite a few spankings from Gilbert that summer and was equal to a much sharper correction than Malcolm choose to give her just then.

Bettie took her spanking like the passionate girl that she was and rode his knee so hard that she left a wet spot behind when she was finally let up. He only stopped when her bottom became tinged with magenta from his palm, though Bettie was sure she could have taken much more. She was enjoying a rapturous fantasy of being the naughty adopted daughter of a strict, handsome father. This enchanting daydream was so powerful that combined with his sound style of spanking, Bettie very nearly succumbed to a climax. When he did let her go she was shaky and gasping for breath. She leaned against him on the bed and let him stroke her hair.

"That was so wonderful," she whispered, making Malcolm very happy. He suddenly felt part of things in Random Point as he had never done before. A knock on the door interrupted their innocent embrace.

William Random entered. Malcolm gave Bettie a kiss on the cheek and strode out of the room. William closed the door behind him and locked it.

"Bettie Brandon, what have you been up to?" William demanded, looking around the room for a perfect platform from which to mount his scene with Bettie.

"Oh, nothing," she smiled.

"That's not what I heard coming up the stairs," William pointed out.

"Mr. Branwell gave me a spanking," Bettie admitted, because there was no point in denying it.

"I understand that you've been reading The Fountainhead."

"Yes, I've just finished it."

"That book influenced me profoundly," William revealed. "I read it when I was fourteen and it made me decide to become an architect."

"How wonderful!" Bettie forgot her embarrassment and beamed at him. "But, in retrospect, what do you think of the book?" she asked in a troubled voice, remembering Gilbert's opinion.

"Oh, I out grew Ayn Rand in college," William admitted, "but she did write a terrific sex scene, didn't she?"

"Oh yes, just divine," Bettie agreed.

"Too bad Howard Roark never turned that spoiled Dominique Francon over his knee."

William found the only armless chair the room contained and casually repositioned it in the center of the room. "Come over here, young lady," he said, sitting down, "and if you have as good an imagination as I suspect you do, you can pretend you're Dominique while you're getting your spanking."

Meanwhile, the last guest had just arrived. Susan led Gilbert into the drawing room where Laura, Michael, Marguerite, Malcolm and Hugo remained. Anthony and Damaris were submerged in the wine cellar and producing distinctive spanking noises at the moment of Gilbert's entry.

"What in the world is going on here?" Gilbert wanted to know.

"Where's Bettie?"

"Bettie is enjoying her farewell party, darling," Marguerite explained, handing him a glass of champagne, which he thanked her for but set down. Gilbert was introduced around the circle. Though the young man attempted polite conversation for a couple of minutes, he was obviously distracted by the thought of Bettie in someone else's hands.

"So, are you Bettie's boyfriend?" Susan boldly queried.

"Yes, Susan, didn't I tell you?" Hugo answered for Gilbert, who had bristled at being questioned quite so confidently by the pony-tailed blonde, "Little Bettie answered Gilbert's ad in the magazine."

"Lucky Gilbert," Susan said, though that young man wasn't completely certain he agreed with this assessment if at that moment his little Bettie was happily prone across someone else's lap!

"What do you want to drink, Gilbert?" Hugo asked soothingly.

"Scotch over ice. Thanks." Gilbert distinctly heard spanking noises coming from above, in the precise direction of Bettie's attic room.

"You're not upset that Bettie's playing, are you?" Susan prodded him gleefully, for Bettie had given her new friend a well-balanced sketch of Gilbert's personality.

"No, I'm not upset," Gilbert lied, "just surprised." He then sat down in a wing chair with his drink to muse. Susan pulled up a hassock and sat on it before him, happy to taunt the handsome boy until he began to pay attention to her.

"Really? Because to me it looks exactly as though you're burning with jealousy," she observed.

"Hardly," Gilbert replied haughtily, "and kindly refrain from quoting phrases from the Harlequin romance library to me." But he now paused to take in every aspect of the Susan package. Her mouth was berry red, a little denim dress flattered her petite torso and sexy clogs exposed her pink heels. Her goldenrod hair rippled down to her waist and her eyes were full of antics.

"So, you say this is – what kind of party?" he suddenly asked.

"Well, it's a party for spanking people only," Susan explained, unwilling to introduce the Bettie theme again so soon.

"I see. I'd read about such events but never believed they really happened."

"Well, they don't happen every day of the week." They both listened to the sounds filtering through the very old house from the bedroom above them.

"Susan is very tempting," thought Gilbert, "but if I play with her I'll become as much of a slut as Bettie is and thereby lose my place on the moral high ground." But what would that matter, he bitterly reflected, if these charmingly dangerous people were to kidnap her away from him her with perverse promiscuity for it's own sake, sans relationships or responsibility.

Finally Susan abandoned the distracted Gilbert, wandering into the kitchen to hunt for fresh cigarettes. In a moment he followed her. "What's keeping Elizabeth so long?" he wondered aloud.

"She's playing with my ex-brother-in-law, William Random, and he has that well known tireless arm," Susan carelessly replied, on the verge of becoming bored with Gilbert, though she could naturally see his appeal for a girl of Bettie's age. "He's only her second partner so far," Susan added, "but others are waiting."

"Isn't that a bit excessive?" Gilbert stiffened with horror at the specter of so many men handling Bettie.

"Delightfully so, I should think," said Susan, from the prospective of one who was enjoying similar attentions that night.

"Well, I don't agree."

"No? What do you think about it?"

"I think that Elizabeth doesn't need or want me here tonight and that maybe I should go before she comes down."

"Oh, Gilbert, surely you can't be so predictably possessive!" Susan was alarmed by his pique. "You were invited to this party too, you know. Without you we have an uneven number of men and women and that will never do. Now that you're here, you must stay. Furthermore, you are obliged to play with at least a couple of women. I myself, being closest to your age, am the logical first choice."

"Is that so?"

"Besides, how can you resist staying, if only to enact the inevitable scene at the end of the night with your little darling?"

"I'd be surprised if she remembered my name after all of you get through with her," Gilbert declared, still vaguely unwilling to be coaxed out of his grouchiness.

"I'm sure you'll make her remember it before you get through with her," Susan returned, once again becoming annoyed by Gilbert's obstinacy.

"You know, you smoke too much," Gilbert said, lighting her next cigarette. "Are you nervous or insecure?"

"Plenty of both," Susan smiled.

"So, you're saying that you're available to play with, right now?"

"Me? You think you might want to play with me?"

"You certainly seem as though you could benefit from a good spanking."

"If it's truly a good one, I probably could."

"Oh? And how would you define a good one?"

"Oh, not too hard, but still sound."

"I think I can provide that," he said. "But where should we go?"

"There's no one here," she suggested, eyeing a heavy, armless wooden chair.

"But suppose someone should walk in?"

"I don't mind, do you?"

"Not if you don't."

Susan waited for him to sit down and approached him from his right hand side. He took her by the arm and pulled her over his lap in one movement, for she was very lithe, though not quite so delicate as Bettie.

"You're quite bold, young lady," Gilbert said, smoothing down her skirt, "I'm not sure I like that."

"Come on, you're used to the female sharks of the Harvard Business School. Comparatively, I'm from the soft toy department at F.A.O. Schwartz."

"I see you've got an answer for everything," he observed, tightening his grip on her waist. "So I'll skip the scolding and get straight to the correction." And with that he began to spank her.

But Gilbert had not landed more than 20 satisfying smacks on the well-rounded seat of her skirt when the door to the wine cellar opened to admit Anthony Newton and Damaris Flagg into the kitchen.

The encounter below, which had gradually, passionately and to their mutual surprise, morphed into Anthony sodomizing Damaris while she was bent over the table, had left the brunette deeply flushed. She hadn't expected to climax in the two minutes he was in her and she was still trembling from it.

Such a radical yet casual sex act had never occurred at one of the parties before and both Damaris and Anthony felt deeply grateful to the gods of love for shielding them from intruders during the most crucial moments of the adventure. What Anthony and Damaris did not know was that the trestle table in Hugo's wine cellar was under an enchantment and ever fated to inspire acts of unbridled lust in whomsoever chanced to bend their partner over it.

At the sight of Susan, Anthony released Damaris' hand and threw the dark haired girl a meaningful glance. Damaris knew that Susan Ross was Anthony's lover and realized that she must act perfectly normal before her or she'd guess in an instant that something momentous had happened. Luckily Susan was so absorbed in the spanking from the new boy that she barely looked up to acknowledge the couple passing through the kitchen. Anthony read this as a signal not to disturb his lover's scene with banter or encouragement and took back the hand of Damaris to quietly lead her from the room and let Gilbert continue with his job.

Gilbert had stopped spanking with his hand in mid-air as Anthony and Damaris passed through the room, but continued before they were out the door again, beginning to enjoy this novel experience greatly.

It was difficult to conceive of a beautiful young lady consenting to be turned over his knee within two minutes of conversation simply because they both happened to be at the same party, and that revelation preoccupied him for some minutes as he increased the tempo and severity of his palm descending on her round, compact bottom.

And yet, Gilbert's mind and heart were so full of Bettie that even as he spanked the beautiful Susan, he could only think of the waywardness of Bettie and how she ought to be the one getting spanked by him, only much harder.

"Ouch!" cried Susan finally, when the spanking became just about as hard as she cared for. This protest awoke Gilbert from his reverie of punishing Bettie and he let Susan up with an abashed apology.

"I'm sorry if that was too hard," he said sincerely, gently setting her skirt to rights for her. "Thank you."

"Thank you," Susan smiled, giving him a hug. "You give a very good spanking."

Bettie had received an even sounder spanking from William Random than she had from Malcolm Branwell, and was enjoying being slowly and deeply masturbated across William's lap when the next knock came on her door.

"It's Hugo," said the voice from without. William quickly ceased to probe Bettie and in fact pulled her panties back up and her skirt back down while Bettie answered, "Just a minute, Hugo."

She was dizzy when she stood up so William made her sit down and went to let Hugo in himself.

"Gilbert arrived about ten minutes ago, Bettie," Hugo informed the surprised girl, "so I thought I'd come up and give you that spanking I promised you before he made his way up here."

William kissed Bettie chastely good-bye and exhorted her to write him after she got to California.

Still dazed by the sensations she had received across William's lap, Bettie was now pulled across Hugo's. As he pulled down her panties to examine the condition of her twice-spanked bottom, Hugo wondered what type of approach would be appropriate for this sweet young lady. He couldn't think of a single naughty thing she had done all summer, except for when she'd called him pussywhipped.

"About that impertinent remark, young lady," he said, running his hand across her warm bottom, which had been tinged a dark rose from the spankings she had already received.

"What remark?" she asked, knowing full well which one he meant.

"A certain vulgar phrase, I'm sure you remember."

"Oh, that remark. I do apologize for that, Hugo," she hastened to reply.

"You'll never know how much restraint I exercised in not taking you over my knee that night."

"I'm sorry."

"Unluckily for you, I never forget an insult." Smack! Smack! His hand came down hard eight more times in a row.

"Oh dear! I said I was sorry!" she wailed, wriggling on his lap.

"Hold still," he ordered. "You need to be taught to speak civilly to your elders." Hugo then began to spank her hard and fast. This was not very pleasant and she tried to get away. But little Bettie wasn't going anywhere and the sounds that soon began to issue from the room were a series of distressed whimpers and finally, shocked sobs. So this was what a punishment spanking felt like! Bettie didn't think she liked it.

"I'm truly sorry!" she begged, quite eager to escape Hugo's relentless grasp and rapidly striking hand.

"From now on, when someone tells you they can't play, for whatever reason, you will respond in a respectful and ladylike manner," Hugo advised, bringing the spanking to a close.

But he didn't let her up right away. Instead, he kept her across his lap for a few minutes, to rub the sting away. This treatment soon had her panting instead of sobbing and Hugo took the opportunity to pull off her panties entirely, make her straddle one of his thighs and lightly spank her flowerlike sex as she spread herself for his hand. Seeing how aroused Bettie instantly became, Hugo pulled her up by the hips a little higher, to expose her Venus mound to the palm of his hand and again began to lightly spank her between her legs, an area already slick and fragrant with her steadily building excitement. Hugo wrapped his arm around her waist and lifted her ever so slightly, to more fully expose her dewy charms.

Bettie could do little more than cry, "Oh! Oh!" as his palm spanked her tiny, throbbing pussy over and over again. This felt so delicious that she never wanted the treatment to end. She hadn't thought much of Hugo's overly harsh spanking, but this was delightful.

Now he stopped spanking her and pressed his palm against her slick, slightly parted labia. She pushed and ground against it like a girl on the verge of an orgasm. At this juncture that Hugo decided to let her go. Better to send her to Gilbert on the brink than satisfied.

"Now you mind you behave nicely to Gilbert," he warned her, helping her to set her clothes to rights.

"He thinks he owns me!" Bettie protested resentfully.

"Oh, nonsense. Gilbert will watch over you and make your life easier when you get to L.A.," Hugo reminded her practically. "Besides, you've been letting him have you all summer, so you must be pretty fond of the boy."

"I suppose I am," she admitted, not enjoying being lectured, even by Hugo. They left her room together and rejoined several of the others in the drawing room. Now Anthony was back in his accustomed position behind the piano with Damaris sitting innocently beside him turning the pages of his music. Marguerite was mixing a cocktail for Michael, with whom she was flirting. Susan and Gilbert sat together, but he jumped to his feet the instant Bettie entered with Hugo, flashing her a look that immediately brought the color to her face.

"Hi, Gilbert," Bettie said unsteadily.

"Elizabeth."

"Have you been here long?"

"Long enough. Let's go into the garden," he took her by the hand and led her out the French doors to the stone bench in the garden.

"What's the matter, Gilbert? You look upset."

"Bettie, why didn't you tell me this was the kind of party you were having tonight?"

"I just found out this afternoon. I didn't even know Hugo had invited you."

"Oh! I see. And I'm sure you would have been just as happy if I'd never shown up!"

"Only if you're going to be horrid."

"So that's the way it is, is it?" he folded his arms.

"Oh, Gilbert, don't you dare strike an attitude. This is my going-away party and I'm going to enjoy it!" she sprung up.

"Elizabeth, I want to know how you feel about me, right now," he grabbed her by the wrist and pulled her down again.

"Gilbert, I like you a lot," she admitted.

"Just like? Not love?"

"I don't know."

"Come on, I never heard of a girl who didn't know when she was in love."

"If I say yes does that mean I can't play with anyone else?"

"That's exactly right," he declared.

"Then the answer is no!" she replied with spirit and flounced back into the house.

Gilbert cursed himself all the way back to Boston for giving Bettie the ridiculous ultimatum. Was he insane trying to pressure a child into making a commitment? And not just any radiantly beautiful child, but Hugo Sands' niece, a very princess of the spanking scene. Had he forgotten every lesson of diplomacy he'd ever learned? It was a miracle she hadn't had Hugo throw him out of the house.

Gilbert was able to twist himself into knots imagining the many handsome, older men Hugo had invited to the party taking turns at fascinating Bettie. How badly he must have compared. He was half way back to Boston before he realized that he should have never left he party, but stayed to play with all the other ladies instead. Then maybe he would have a fighting chance of arousing some hint of jealousy in Bettie's perfect little bosom.

But Gilbert's was an optimistic nature. He still had the advantage of having her virtually to himself in California. She was sure to be lonely there and he was sure to compare favorably with the kids in the dorm. Unless, of course, Hugo supplied her with contacts ahead of time, which as Gilbert thought about it, seemed only inevitable. Now Gilbert became gloomy again. With Hugo as her ally, how could he ever hope to isolate her affections?

When he walked into his apartment, nearly defeated, he was greeted by a message from Bettie, left rather breathlessly, only moments before his arrival home. "Gilbert?" she stammered charmingly, causing his heart to pound violently, "I guess you're not home yet. It's Elizabeth... Well, I just wanted to say that I'm sorry I was so contrary tonight. It was just the excitement of the party. Of course I love you. And I can't wait to see you in L.A. So don't be mad at me. Okay? Bye, Gilbert!"

Gilbert smiled.

Chapter Three

The Difficult Seduction

Teresa Clifford at 36 was single, happy and well adjusted to this state. Thanks to the patronage of a wealthy New Yorker, the L.A.-based cartoonist and part time fetish model led a carefree existence and wanted for nothing.

She met Augie Rose for the first time at a party in Beverly Glen, to which she found her way in the company of screen writer Carter Webster and his girlfriend Aurora Milne, both friends of Teresa's patron, the musical composer Anthony Newton.

Teresa was immediately drawn to their hostess Lucy Burke, a young blonde in a cherry leather bustier dress and fetish pumps. Lucy had the look of a co-conspirator, a Gwen to Teresa's U-69, a gorgeous, salon-pampered creature to tie up, tease, and whip until her arm got tired. Meanwhile, Lucy scanned Teresa's outfit and visibly melted, for Teresa wore a black leather cat suit, high collared in back and unzipped to show cleavage in front, with her silky, black hair down her back. Five inch-heeled boots from London gave her extra stature and power.

"What a perfect woman," said Lucy, taking one of Teresa's gauntleted hands and squeezing it. "Who are you?"

Teresa introduced herself.

"But, of course you're a mistress?" Lucy breathed with admiration.

"Not exactly," Teresa smiled and explained about her hundred video roles.

"I'd love to see your films!" cried Lucy.

"I'll send you one."

"Thanks!"

Lucy led Teresa over to the buffet and poured her a glass of champagne. Teresa unselfconsciously filled a plate with dainty items, exchanging a smile now and then with Lucy, who lingered by her, quiet with admiration but eager to learn more about her guest.

"You're very charming," said Teresa. "I'd love to have you as my victim in a video."

"That would be delicious!" said Lucy with excitement. "But Crossjay would have the vapors if I did anything so exhibitionistic."

"Crossjay?"

"My significant other," Lucy indicated a blond, bronzed monolith in an Armani suit that leaned against the mantelpiece, nursed a white wine and glowered at any man who came near Lucy. "He thinks we're getting married some day and he wants me to behave in case he ever goes into politics."

"He's very attractive, in an uptight, scary, right wing conservative way," Teresa commented, smiling ever so slightly at Crossjay, who returned a suspicious glance.

"Isn't he though?" replied Lucy fondly, waving at Crossjay, who'd been brooding on the tightness of her dress all night.

He had tried to make her put on something less alarming. But her will to be seen in her new North Beach Leather outfit prevailed. She might let him dictate what she wore at Republican fundraisers, but her own scene party was quite another matter.

He had taken her over his knee, in his usual style, but after five minutes of hard smacking on his part and stubborn non-compliance on hers, he realized that he could not hope to change her mind in the time left to dress before the party. He let her go and warned her that she would be caned for her insolence later.

Lucy had heard this threat before and wondered whether Crossjay even owned a cane. If he didn't, she resolved to find him one. Meanwhile, she had found a worthy new friend in Teresa Clifford.

Approaching the buffet from the other side at the same moment was Carter Webster and his friend, Augie Rose.

"The thing I hate about parties like this is how easily pros manage to sneak in," commented Augie of a rather obvious mistress as he filled fresh pastry puffs with pate. Lucy and Teresa's backs were turned but they both stiffened at these words, Lucy blushing with embarrassment. Both girls turned to look at the offender, who was blithely unaware of his audience.

"My girlfriend used to do sessions, you know," Carter admonished the pulp fiction publisher firmly.

"Aurora is a perfect angel and a total aberration in the L.A. scene," Augie protested vigorously, finally raising his penetrating eyes to meet Teresa's narrowing ones across the buffet.

"Hi," he said immediately, "have we met? Augie Rose," he extended his hand across the buffet towards Teresa. Teresa looked at him briefly then turned on her heel and walked away.

"Wasn't she rude?" Augie complained to Carter in surprise.

"She probably heard what you just said about pros."

"Don't tell me she's one?" Augie flushed darkly under his tan. He looked at Teresa again and noted every detail of her outfit, particularly the stiletto-heeled boots, which gave her high, firm bottom an additional lift.

"Who is that fabulous woman?"

"Her name's Teresa Clifford, and among other things, she's Anthony Newton's protégé."

"You mean she's being kept by him?"

"I believe she wants for nothing."

"So what's her story? Is she a high-priced call girl, or what?"

"I don't think you could have her at any price after what she heard you say," observed Carter with amusement.

"Nonsense, my specialty is getting back into women's good graces. I start with a beautiful letter, explaining all my faults. Works every time. Tell me some more about her."

"I don't know if I should. She is a personal friend of mine and frankly you don't deserve her," Carter replied. "But just so you don't go insulting her again, she's not a call girl, she's a player, and an actress. I'm surprised you didn't recognize her."

Teresa put as much distance between herself and the offensive party guest as she could before sitting down to her plate out by the pool. "Of course, he'd never have need of a pro," she brooded, remembering the angular grace of the man in the grey, sharkskin suit.

"Unless he's a submissive," she mused. "In which case he's probably bitter about being bled white by an extravagant mistress."

Teresa finished her snack, lit a cigarette and took up her champagne glass to further ponder the arrogant snob she'd just met. Discovering whether he was dominant or submissive would tend to put his remark into perspective. And it would also guide her future discourse with the problematical man. For she could tell from the look he had flashed her as she walked away that he would not leave well enough alone. His eyes betrayed his desires as quickly as a remote control changed channels.

And sure enough, the next thing she knew, he was looming above her on the terrace, asking to be allowed to sit down.

"Sure," she said indifferently. He pulled a chair up to the table beside her and lit his own cigarette.

"I'm trying to quit," he confided.

"Me too. I'm down to about five a day."

"That's outstanding. I wish I could claim that much progress," Augie confessed.

"Are you just a ball of nerves?" Teresa asked sympathetically.

"How did you know?"

"You seem tense."

"You're very perceptive," Augie was encouraged by her friendliness. His shoulders visibly relaxed. He was 6'1", and wiry, with a long and not unpleasant face. His dark brown hair was short and straight and he had a wide mouth that was quick to smile and smirk.

"Why are you so tense, Mr. Rose?"

"Well, Miss Clifford, it's because I value your good opinion and I'm afraid that I've lost it forever."

"Why should you value my good opinion?"

"When a man meets a beautiful woman he wants her to think well of him."

"I couldn't possibly think well of a man who was so prejudiced against honest, working women," Teresa let her polite facade slip at last as she downed her champagne and strode back into the house.

"Okay, she told me off," Augie thought, following her in, "she's gotten it out of her system. She'll be slightly embarrassed and a lot nicer the next time I confront her." In the hall he checked his tie and hair in the mirror.

Augie was a great believer in synchronicity and every other variety of New Age nonsense that suited his plans at any given moment, and he was firmly convinced that he had met and antagonized Teresa Clifford for a reason. Augie picked his parties carefully and considered the proper object of each one either cementing a deal or going home with an interesting woman.

Teresa Clifford was self-contained and intriguing. The remark about pros had been unfortunate, he acknowledged, but he certainly never meant it to apply to artistes like herself. Augie wasn't quite aware just yet of what Teresa actually did, although he determined to become acquainted with her work immediately. For all he cared she might have done a bubble dance in a pink leotard. The look in her eyes was what stayed with him.

Augie Rose was the scion of a rich New York delicatessen family who had come out to Los Angeles ten years before to start a career in publishing. Immediate diversification and an on-going commitment to relentless production, regardless of quality, had been largely responsible for his current success. Augie's publishing standards were low, his output high. He made a good deal of money but his company was always on the edge of collapse. He paid his staff well, advertised widely and traveled frequently. He had a million dollar credit line that was always extended to the limit. But he didn't owe back taxes and all of his addictions were legal.

Augie Rose was 38 years old. He lived high and supported several ex-wives, by whom he was well liked. He was in therapy, had a personal trainer, enjoyed shopping and considered himself to be very nearly happy.

Augie Rose was in the scene and always had been. It had started off with a simple spanking fixation and had stayed that way for years. But in coming out to California, his tastes had broadened as his curiosity increased about the mysterious world of B&D. Now he was convinced that he was not just a top, but also cherished a romantic notion of being a master.

Augie's bedroom dominance had led to the eventual break up of his two marriages. He couldn't seem to interest either wife in playing and the older he became; the stronger his need to experience this side of his sexuality grew.

After the second divorce, just the year before, he had discovered the scene and had been searching within it ever since for a woman to fall in love with.

Augie had restricted his activities exclusively to a membership in the local B&D support group, which was where he had met Crossjay and Lucy. Meeting Lucy had given Augie hope. Even though she was taken, the fact that she existed at all was encouraging. The problem with the support group was that it contained mostly couples. Meeting single submissives was the difficult part. Crossjay kept advising him to try the personal ads, which was how he had found Lucy, but as with most things that seemed too easy, Augie was skeptical.

Augie met many women in his work and had more female friends than the average gay male. His secretary, therapist and personal trainer were all women. And surrounded by the women of Beverly Hills, Augie was never without a dinner date. But so far he hadn't found what he really longed for, a woman of style who played in the scene. Every time a woman he dated with wore leather, his heart leapt, but it never came to anything but wardrobe.

Teresa was obviously different. She seemed to be exactly the kind of girl he was looking for, except for being a pro, which he now found he couldn't care less about.

As the evening progressed, Teresa and Lucy found a way to be alone. However, no sooner had they found themselves a room in which to play than the spanking sounds which shortly issued from it instantly attracted several voyeurs, who rudely burst in upon them without bothering to knock. The intruders included Crossjay, who was jealous of everyone who wanted to play with Lucy, and Augie, who was thrilled to find Teresa again.

Teresa looked up from her happy job to calmly confront the men. Crossjay said, "Carry on," almost pleasantly, but folded his arms and leaned against a dresser to watch Teresa complete her task under his suspicious eye. Augie lightly dropped into an armchair.

"Actually, I had finished," said Teresa coolly, delighted to deprive

Mr. Rose of a free show. Crossjay was content to reclaim Lucy and give her a shake for going off to play without letting him know.

"Why don't you just put her on a tether?" Teresa suggested.

Lucy laughed and Crossjay flushed. Had she been anyone other than Teresa Clifford, protégé of one of his wealthiest clients, Crossjay might have thrown her out of the house for her impertinence.

"Miss Clifford?" he asked with a smile, "may we play?"

Teresa's tummy fluttered as she looked up at the tall, blond, surf-bred Viking of a male. Surely he was only annoyed and not really angry, she wondered, looking at Lucy for a sign. Lucy nodded her head with an irrepressible smile.

"I wonder what Anthony would advise," thought Teresa. Then she remembered that Anthony was the one who had told her about this party, and might, in fact, hope that she made a good impression on her host and hostess.

"Of course," Teresa replied after only a moment's hesitation. "But in private!" she stipulated, still quite unwilling to perform for the benefit of Augie, or for that matter, Lucy.

"Fine!" Crossjay said agreeably, taking her by the hand and pulling her out of the room and down the corridor to his bedroom, which was as masterful a room as she had ever seen. He locked the door.

"So, let's talk a little first," she said shakily, retreating behind the enormous wooden bed.

"Very well," he said, removing his jacket, "talk away."

"Listen, if you're really mad at me for what I said, I'm not going to play!" Teresa protested stubbornly, folding her slender arms and standing her ground.

Crossjay finished rolling up his sleeves, then took her by the arm, sat on the edge of the bed and turned her over his knee.

He landed a few medium hard smacks across her perfect, though heavily protected bottom before examining the smooth seat of her cat suit for a zipper or some other avenue of entry, but to no avail. The garment was front zipping and one piece. To console himself, Crossjay smacked Teresa a good deal harder than he might have done, had her beautiful bottom been more accessible.

Teresa took the spanking like the lively, bouncy player she was, wriggling and kicking and struggling just enough to make him work a bit to hold her in place, at least initially, but not enough to actually break free. As soon as Crossjay pulled her over his lap Teresa realized why Lucy was so taken with the country club lummox. He had a vastly comfortable lap, a big, warm, well-padded hand and a way of holding one that controlled and embraced all at once.

"I have a hard enough time keeping Lucy out of trouble," Crossjay complained suddenly between spates of smacks. "I don't need you to agitate her even more."

"Now that we've been formally introduced, you have no idea what kind of trouble Lucy and I are going to get up to together," Teresa promised, with a complete lack of concern. This remark earned Teresa a very sound spanking that went on long enough to torture Augie almost to death as he heard it from down the hall.

Crossjay only spanked Teresa until his arm got tired. In about twenty minutes, he let her up. She sat straight back down on his lap to steady her shaky limbs for a moment and while she was there, put her arms around his neck. Crossjay tightened his arms around Teresa's waist and buried his face in her long, black hair. "I suppose you're all right," he murmured.

"Get used to me. Lucy is just my kind of girlfriend," Teresa promised.

Crossjay groaned at the thought of this powerful new tag team while Teresa kissed his smooth cheek and wriggled on his lap. He tightened his arms around her again; loathe to release her now that she had started to grind against his erection.

"Do you think he's waiting for me?" Teresa suddenly asked, jumping off Crossjay's lap and going to fix her hair in a mirror.

"Augie Rose?" Now Crossjay straightened his tie in the mirror, rolled down his sleeves again and put his jacket back on.

"I don't like him," she said, unconsciously rubbing her bottom through her pants. Crossjay's spanking would stay with her for some time.

"Oh, Augie's not so bad," Crossjay said of his client and racquet-ball buddy.

"I think he's very rude," Teresa declared, allowing Crossjay to open the door for her.

"Look who's talking. I would have spanked you more severely for your freshness, except for the fact that your hard little bottom hurt my hand," he complained as they went in search of the others.

A stroll through the upstairs hall brought familiar faces into view inside every door. Teresa suddenly realized why Augie had pros on the brain, for the house was filled with real Hollywood players, half of whom worked in the B&D industry, either in the film or service end. Some of them were brilliant in thousand dollar ensembles, others tacky, in cheap or worn-out fetish finery, but nearly all of them were real in their way.

Lucy had a pipeline into the L.A. scene (Crossjay suspected a notorious mistress!) through which she had managed to meet everyone over the last year. Crossjay really wasn't sure that he liked this, but as with most of the mischief Lucy got up to, there wasn't a thing he could do about it, except thrash her for it, which he frequently did.

Meanwhile, encouraged by the ease with which Teresa had accepted Crossjay's invitation to play, Augie had been waiting for her to re-emerge. He strode to meet her, and fell into step with her as she started down the stairs.

"I hope you aren't leaving," he said.

"I think I am," she replied, pleasantly enough.

"Look, can we trade cards?" he pressed his into her hand.

"I'm sorry," she said, "I'm not carrying one." But he watched her slip his into her purse.

"Let me write your number down, then," he said, whipping out a pen and a small notebook.

"Why?" she asked.

"Because I want to call you."

"Why?"

"Because I find you very –" he groped for a word that might not sound patronizing – "appealing."

Teresa smiled slightly but shook her head and continued on her way out of the house. Augie followed her outside.

"Oh, I just remembered," she cried, "I came with Carter and

Aurora!" She turned to re-enter the house but he stopped her.

"Let me drive you home," he suggested.

"Oh, very well, but I'll have to tell them I'm leaving," she again tried to re-enter the house.

"I'll tell them," he offered, "you just stay out here and have a nice cigarette." This sounded both civilized and sensible and Teresa accepted, longing to sit in one of the veranda chairs and rest her feet, which had been in the very high heels for hours. He was back before she finished her smoke and ushered her into a new Mercedes convertible the next moment.

"What is your orientation, anyway?" she asked, not finding it hard to get comfortable beside him.

"I'm a master," he answered, though not emphatically.

"Oh, I see," she replied with a smile. "But, I'm sure you don't think I'm a slave!"

"I saw you go off and play with Crossjay and it didn't sound like he was the one getting it."

"Oh, I love spanking, but that's as submissive as I get."

"That's as submissive as you ever need to get."

"But you said the word master."

"Did I? I meant dominant."

"Did you?"

"Tell me about yourself, Miss Clifford."

"Well, I'm a video actress, a model and I draw a comic strip called Midnight for a number of alternative newspapers."

"You do Midnight?"

"Have you read it?"

"Of course I read it. It's about punks."

"That's the one."

Augie gave her a sidelong glance of new appreciation. "You're very clever."

"Thanks."

"Ever think of putting all the strips into a book? I'm a publisher, you know. We should talk about this."

"What do you publish?"

"Magazines, pulp fiction, exposes, novelizations, self-help books, pamphlets and I just started a new crossword puzzle line."

"A publisher, eh?" Teresa congratulated herself on getting in the car with Augie in spite of a lingering aversion to his initial captiousness. No wonder Anthony had told her to attend this party. This was just the sort of person she needed to meet!

"We really should talk soon. Meanwhile, if you happen to have any juicy memoirs lying around that one of my editors can slam onto a floppy, dig them out before we meet again. You'd be amazed at how fast I can get a book to press."

"You mean B&D related?"

"The racier the better," he advised sagely.

"Oh, turn left at the bottom of the hill; I live a block from Beverly Hills High," Teresa instructed Augie.

"So, will you call me?" he asked, pulling up to the garden apartments where she lived.

"Sure," she said, getting out of the car.

"Wait a minute," he said, "do we really have to separate so soon?"

Teresa stood on the curb and appraised him afresh in the mellow glow of an old fashioned street lamp. Understanding she was making a decision, Augie's heart began to pound violently.

"Come up for a drink," Teresa replied, then turned on her heel and preceded him up the walkway.

Teresa had a smartly furnished duplex apartment decorated with her own art and numerous, handsomely mounted fetish photographs. Augie examined the provocative portraits of Teresa that lined the walls as she mixed the vodka tonic he requested.

"Show me one of your videos," he asked peremptorily.

"What kind would you like to see? I've played dom, sub and switch." Teresa was not at all reluctant to exhibit her work. Like most performers, she enjoyed admiration.

"Pick your favorite one," he told her, accepting the drink and settling into a chair opposite the VCR. He couldn't help but notice the several framed portraits of Anthony Newton which also hung in her portrait gallery and felt that familiar twinge of unease that always came upon him when he was about to seduce another man's woman. It was not enough to stop him from laying plans, but it wasn't an enjoyable sensation.

Teresa was happy to change clothes while he watched the tape she selected. She knew the video would give him ideas, but she wanted him to see her at her most disarming. It was a fantasy about a woman (Teresa) who seduces her therapist (some not-half-bad young actor) into spanking her. The script was witty and Teresa fairly brimming with animal spirits as she portrayed a mischievous girl.

Augie was very impressed and a good deal more respectful the next time she appeared before him, having changed into a white denim dress that went perfectly with her ponytail and the cute clogs that punctuated her long legs. He noticed that she had gone from totally zipped up to completely accessible, from black to white, and wondered if this transformation was too obscure to be read as an invitation.

"You're sensational," he told her, as she turned off the tape, feeling he had seen enough for the moment. "I didn't know fetish videos had gotten this good."

"Thanks."

"You're really awfully talented."

"Thanks."

"Listen, about that pro remark you overheard," he began, with a rising color, "I want to apologize for that."

Teresa shrugged. "It doesn't matter."

"It does. What's it going to take for you to forgive me?"

"Why should you care what I think?"

"You know, you're not making this altogether easy for me," Augie finally growled.

"Have you ever paid to see a submissive?"

"No."

"So what do you know about pros to make you so contemptuous of them?"

"Nothing."

"Well, I think that just to teach you a lesson, I'm going to require you to go to a club and pay to do a session."

"What's this you're saying, now?"

"You heard me."

"You're giving me an ultimatum?"

"Uh-huh," said Teresa, handing him her bottle of white wine to uncork for her with a complete lack of concern.

"Suppose I comply, what happens then?"

Teresa was finally beginning to have fun with Augie. "What happens after you comply with my instructions? Why, then you get forgiven."

"Well, I think it's absurd," he expressed indignantly. "I've apologized and that will have to do. Unless of course you wish to volunteer to be this pro who gets the whipping?"

"Me? Oh, no. I don't do that anymore."

"Is that so?"

"I mean, I only play for fun now."

"Then I don't see why you took exception to my remark."

"Because I used to do sessions and it hurt my feelings. You think you're better than women who play at B&D for a living. Why?"

"I don't think I'm better."

"You're arrogant and horrid."

Augie sighed. "In time you'll see I'm not."

"Oh, very well, I'm prepared to take your word for that because you've been behaving in a fairly civilized manner this last hour, but if you aren't willing to comply with my suggestion, how do you intend to elevate yourself in my esteem?"

"I'm prepared to offer you a book contract."

"Sounds as though you're trying to buy my forgiveness."

"Whatever it takes, by all means."

"You know, I may have misjudged you. You're not completely terrible."

"Have some more wine," he poured for her, "I improve with alcohol."

Teresa laughed but realized that she was becoming altogether too relaxed.

"You'd better go now," she suddenly said, unwilling to submit to him so soon.

"Well, thank you for letting me visit." He stood up immediately. She walked him to the door. He shook her hand goodbye, then kissed her lightly on the cheek. The next moment he was gone.

The following day Teresa received a bouquet of pink and white tea roses, two tickets for the upcoming Sex Pistols concert and the following letter:

Dear Teresa,

Thanks for the drink and private screening. You're exciting and I want to know you better. Only I'm afraid that you don't like me because of the initial bad impression I made on you. Being famished made me cranky and subsequently rude. Lucy's salmon pate soon revived me, but by that time I had already insulted you. You were really very nice to have me over after that.

Come see the Sex Pistols with me?
> *Hopefully yours,*
> *Augustus Rose*

Teresa felt a queer sensation in the pit of her tummy when she read the letter. Teresa thought, with a smile, "what a ridiculous name."

"What kind of approach does a really intelligent woman appreciate the most?" Augie Rose queried his therapist, Dr. Prudence Carr, the next afternoon.

"If I answer questions like that I'll have to charge you double," his smartly bespectacled doctor purred. "And what would you want with an intelligent woman, anyway?"

Augie didn't mind Dr. Carr's sarcasm or anything else about her. So far she hadn't been able to cure his chronic anxiety, but she had certainly masked it admirably with some marvelous prescription drugs. Also, she was rather lovely in her plain, dressed-down way and had a bewitching voice.

"Or rather," she corrected herself, "what would an intelligent woman want with you?"

"Not to mention the fact," he agreed, "that I'm also thoroughly out-classed by the man who pays her bills."

"So why do you think you have a hope in hell?" Prudence asked pleasantly, amused by the turn of today's session.

Ever since Dr. Carr had prescribed the proper drugs to stop Augie from grinding his teeth at night, there had been little real reason for the expensive therapy to continue. But Augie felt that he had need of her, if only to tell him, from the modern woman's point of view, when he was being a buffoon and where he could improve. He gave her to understand that her job was to polish and refine the rough gem that he knew himself to be; so that when he did chance to encounter an exceptional woman he would be ready to dazzle her with his wisdom and restraint.

This task of civilizing Augie was an on-going job and one that appealed to the fashionable young psychoanalyst. He was one of her few patients who didn't depress or bore her and she secretly admired his good looks and taste.

Augie pillowed his head on his hands and replied, "It's something you wouldn't understand, Prudence."

"Me? Not understand something you could say?" Dr. Carr was amused.

"It has to do with the Scene."

"The Scene? You mean the alternative lifestyle support group you belong to?"

"No, I mean the entire B&D subculture. It's something I've noticed from being at just the few parties I've attended. When a dom and a sub meet, they can't help but imagine what it might be like to play with each other. I think I've got Teresa at that stage right now."

"Well, it might be smart not to rush things. Try to run into each other at a few events before you take her out. Be a refreshing surprise when she least expects you to pop up. Try to get invited to small, intimate parties with mutual friends when you know she'll be there. This will give her a chance to observe your behavior in mixed company on a regular basis and form a better opinion of you than she probably has now. After three or four such encounters I would be surprised if this lady's heart didn't beat a little faster when your signature sunglasses came into view."

"That's excellent advice, Prudence. I'll follow it!"

Teresa of course had no idea that her new admirer would possess such a sage female counselor and thought it quite remarkable when Augie began to pop up all around town. She saw him at an opening on

Melrose, ran into him at Carter Webster's house, suddenly discovered that they went to the same gym and of course, had begun to interface with him on a professional level about her proposed book.

The Sex Pistols concert was still a month away and so far he'd held off on asking for a proper date, though he had bought her either lunch or cappuccino after each meeting and once, uncannily, happened to run into her right outside of North Beach Leather, in time to help her choose and pay for her outfit for the concert. Augie called such phenomena synchronicity, but Teresa knew good planning when she saw it.

Through all of this Teresa kept wondering if and when Augie was going to make a definite move and what it would be like. She was almost certain of him being a ridiculously inept player, in need of many minutes of instruction before producing even a reasonable facsimile of well-bred control. But by week three of knowing Augie Rose, she had fully reversed her original estimation of the high-strung publisher.

And then came the day when she awoke with a start, realizing that she wanted nothing more than to talk to and see Augie Rose, to spend the day and possibly the night with him; to stroll into his cluttered office, push the door closed and boldly sit on his lap. Teresa stretched with pleasure as she realized that she was in love. She was now madly curious to discover what he might be like in the bedroom and hastened to make her will known.

"I simply can't wait until the night of the concert to make love to him," Teresa thought to herself while impatiently listening to his answering machine message.

"Augie?" Teresa asked in a breathless voice, suddenly frightened of the enormity of the invitation she was about to extend. When he didn't pick up she quickly murmured, "It's Teresa Clifford. Please call me when it's convenient." Then she hung up with a throbbing pulse. "What was I thinking?" she wondered. "Was I really going to offer myself to Augie Rose, just like that?"

Teresa remembered she had a shoot that day in Burbank and hastened to redial Augie's number and let him know that she wouldn't be available until much later in the evening.

The video shoot ran ten tedious hours. Teresa arrived home starved and exhausted at eleven p.m. There was one message from Augie saying he'd call back around midnight. Teresa smiled, thinking, "That leaves me more than enough time to shower and dress." Synchronicity again.

When he called at twelve it was from his car, parked outside her door. She ran right down and got into the car. "I've been shooting all day and I'm starved."

"Pantry or Pacific Dining Car?"

"Pantry, please, I don't want to wait very long before I get fed."

"Good. I haven't eaten all day either," he admitted.

"Uh oh! Doesn't that mean we're going to be cranky?"

"Never with you."

"Really? I'm almost disappointed."

"Why?" Augie smiled his big, wide smile at her.

"I don't know, why do you think?"

Augie gave her a sidelong glance, realizing with a start that for the first time she almost seemed to be flirting with him. In fact, she seemed to be smiling in such a way that indicated pleasure simply at being in his company.

"What are you looking so pleased about?" he demanded.

"I don't know."

"You sounded slightly urgent when you called me today, why?"

"That was so long ago I can't even remember," she replied staring out at passing Beverly Hills.

"I think that's the first time you ever called me," he observed.

"Was it?"

"What made me pop into your head today?"

"I don't know."

"It couldn't possibly be that you're starting to like me?"

Teresa only smiled.

"Tell me all about how you like to play," she urged him as they awaited their steaks across a very plain table in an ancient room with sawdust on the floor.

"I can't talk about a thing like that here," Augie protested. "Why I can barely talk about it with my analyst."

"You're so neurotic that you need an analyst?" Teresa was disconcerted by this news.

"We say co-dependent these days, darling, and don't be judgmental. If it weren't for Beverly Hills therapists, five Mercedes dealers wouldn't be putting their kids through Harvard."

"I'm sorry, Augie, you're quite right."

"Don't worry, I just go because I like to talk to Dr. Carr. She cured my nervous disorder within the first week of treatment."

"I'll bet she is very attractive, is she not?"

"Nothing like you, but she's quietly cute. If she were in the scene she would have been wife number three long ago."

"I take it one and two were not?"

"That's right. How about you? Ever been married? Any significant others at the moment?"

"I've never been married. And no, I don't exactly have a boyfriend at the moment."

"But someone does have a claim on you, doesn't he?"

"I wouldn't call it that. And I'm certainly free to pursue any romantic relationships I choose."

"This is very encouraging."

After dinner they went for a windy drive in Malibu Canyon. Teresa felt completely revitalized by the food and fresh, summer night air.

"Want to see where I live?" he asked.

"Sure."

Augie owned a two story white stone cottage in Nichols Canyon set on five acres of wooded property with scenic views and a large swimming pool. A new Range Rover guarded the garage, over which lived the Salvadoran cleaning lady and her husband, who tended the gardens.

The interior of the cottage was bathed in Tuscan hues and exquisitely furnished. "Luxe be a lady tonight," Teresa thought to herself with a smile at host's expensive tastes. Augie was a brilliant businessman, but with less idea of how to live within his means than a girl with her first credit card. They had cocktails on the balcony of his bedroom overlooking the canyon, which was illuminated by a full moon and stars. While Teresa enjoyed the view, Augie suffered torments while trying to decide what to do next and when to do it.

"You were going to tell me about how you enjoy playing," Teresa suddenly reminded him, with merry eyes. But the ever-glib Augie was suddenly seized by a fit of shyness and couldn't bring himself to articulate his desires to the confident Teresa before finishing both his cocktail and hers in a couple of gulps.

"I'm into D&S," he said hesitantly.

"D&S?" Teresa laughed. "Okay, but do you really think you're suited to the dominant role? From what I've observed, you seem to have all the earmarks of a classic submissive."

"And you seem to have none," he observed. "But I still have faith that you'll let me spank you."

"Is that what you'd like to do above all things?"

"For starters."

"And what then?"

"That's up to you," said Augie, taking her by the hand and leading her into his bedroom.

Teresa felt that queer thrill that she always felt when a new man turned her over his knee, but more so. The fact that he was obviously nervous and unsure of himself added piquancy and emotion to this first encounter. She unconsciously tensed for the first hard, jagged blow, for this was what she expected from him. But instead he merely stroked her through her summer dress, enjoying her weight across his lap.

"You don't mind this, do you?" he asked her, lightly patting and stroking her now.

"Oh, no!" She gave a little wriggle on his lap, the tension leaving her body as she realized that Augie was perhaps a bit smoother than expected. Meanwhile Augie felt as though he were about to unwrap the world's most enticing present. For it was clear that she was going to allow him to spank her, with no further questions asked.

He pulled up her skirt to reveal lace trimmed white nylon panties snugly clinging to the perfect alabaster bottom he'd seen in the videos. He caressed her, then began to spank her, somewhat briskly, because he knew she was used to it. It was fun, as he spanked her, to remember how haughty she had been on the first night they met.

"Teresa?" he paused to rub where he had spanked.

"Yes?"

"Remember how fresh you were to me on the night we met?"

"I don't recall being fresh," she said with a secret smile.

"No? You don't remember that self-righteous speech about honest working women?" Smack! Smack! Augie got serious and Teresa caught her breath. "Did it make you feel better to tell me off like that?"

"No. It upset me," she replied truthfully, "I don't like getting angry."

"Then you decided to taunt me by letting Crossjay spank you," Augie reminded her, warming her bottom indignantly at the memory. Teresa whimpered and ground a little against his lap, thrilled to have inspired such long lasting jealousy.

Augie had always felt that playing with the right girl could be very cute. Teresa was simply made for spanking. He warmed her panties for fifteen minutes, intermittently fingering her through them, before pulling them down. By the time he got to the bare bottom portion of the spanking, Teresa was so excited that she couldn't help but arch to his hand, spread her legs, and in every way but verbally communicate her desire for the correction to continue.

Augie spanked Teresa for a long time, hoping to make her climax. Finally it happened, twenty-four minutes into the scene. Augie was glad because her fair skin was stained deeper than magenta by then and he became afraid of marking her. He never dreamed she'd take so much and for so long or allow him so many liberties besides.

His long, deft fingers, pressed deep inside her in two places were impossible not to succumb to, and at length she cried out breathlessly, "Oh, stop!" as the tremors rippled through her.

"Augie!" she said, when he pulled her up and took her in his arms.

"Yes?"

"You made me come."

"It wasn't difficult," he said, pulling back her hair to nuzzle her throat. She shivered against him but deliberately took one of his hands and placed it on her perfect bosom.

"You may take me now," she declared.

Augie did not need to be asked twice.

The affair came to a full boil almost overnight. Augie was in love and with a personality as emotional as his own; this meant extra sessions with Dr. Carr to dissect his ecstatic angst.

"Things seem to be going so well between you and Teresa," Prudence chided him one morning two weeks later, "why must you agitate the waters?"

"I can't help it," Augie insisted, "I've been grinding my teeth at night thinking about this upcoming trip she's taking to New York to see Anthony Newton. And no amount of medicine helps subdue the anxiety."

"Well, of course it doesn't."

"Well, then how do intelligent people deal with the reality of gnawing jealousy?"

"I suppose they just suppress it."

"She says she loves me."

"In two weeks flat? Good for you."

"Doesn't that give me the right to at least ask her to stop being the mistress of this other man?"

"No."

"But if she truly loves me, why shouldn't I depend upon her fidelity?"

"Depend upon her fidelity? Augie, you've been lucky enough to attract the interest of an artist, a free spirit. Don't kill it by smothering her."

"Prudence, you're very smart, but you know nothing whatever about love. Why, I think Teresa would be terribly disappointed if I didn't express my jealousy of her – friend."

"You asked my opinion."

"If you ever get married, don't you intend to be faithful to your husband, Prudence?"

"Sure," she returned pleasantly, "at first." At 32, Prudence had a marriage and several long relationships already behind her and was enjoying an unfettered lifestyle.

"I guess in a way I'm longing for that comfortable, suburban nirvana invented by Madison Avenue in the late fifties. Teresa wears tweed skirts, cashmere cardigans and pearls and drives me to the train station every morning."

"Leaving her ample time for affairs with golf pros, personal trainers and masseurs," said Prudence crushingly.

"Are all smart women as cynical as you?"

"Oh, come on, Augie, you know as well as I do that humans are not monogamous."

"But, Prudence, love should make us wish to be intimate only with the object of our adoration."

"Why?"

"Because that's the nature of love."

"By whose authority?"

"By the authority of the very blood in our veins," Augie decided, dramatically jumping to his feet with excitement. "Damn it, Prudence, I've got to declare myself to Teresa before she goes to New York."

"Do as you think best, but don't give her any ultimatums. She might tell you to go to hell and then it would be embarrassing to call her for a date when she got back."

Augie insisted on driving Teresa to the airport that night to catch the red eye for New York, but said very little on the way. But though he manfully suppressed his anguish at her impending departure, Teresa was not unaware of his pain and confusion at her leaving him to visit Anthony Newton in the city of Augie's origin.

"You don't have to stay with me till I get on the plane, you know," she told him in the terminal bar.

"I know."

"Augie? I'll be back on Monday night."

"Good."

"How much can you miss me in three days?"

"If you liked me half as much as I like you, you'd know."

"Oh, Augie, I do like you! I'll prove how much as soon as I get back."

"How?" Augie was surprised by this promise.

"I've ordered a Catholic school uniform. It should be here by the time I get back."

"That was thoughtful," he said, kissing her inner wrist and feeling soothed.

The last thing Augie Rose expected that melancholy night was to be awakened out of his usual light sleep by a desperate command from Dr. Carr to pick up his phone!

Augie fumbled the receiver into his hand in the dark of his bedroom and noticed that his bedside clock read three a.m.

"Augie? It's Prudence Carr. Are you awake enough to understand me?"

"Yes, Prudence. Is anything the matter?"

"I'm in jail and I need you to come bail me out."

Augie threw on clothes, jumped in his car and brought the thousand dollars bail money she'd requested to the station house where she was being held sixteen minutes after she'd hung up. Ten minutes later she was free and in his arms in the parking lot outside the West Hollywood sheriff's station, sobbing with shame and relief. In a moment he got her into his car and drove her to her high-rise duplex condo in Century City.

On the way she began to sob again, convinced that they intended to keep her impounded BMW convertible on top of revoking her driver's license for six months. Then there was the fine and year of community service she could in all probability look forward to, in addition to a rehab program she would have to enroll in and if this ever got out, a mangled reputation.

"What in the world were you arrested for Prudence?"

"Driving over the speed limit, under the influence of cocaine," the nerve shattered analyst admitted hollowly.

"You?" Augie flashed her a look of amazement as he handed his car to a valet in her underground garage and they walked toward the elevators. Prudence hung her head in misery and trudged into the elevator in a good little black crepe cocktail dress that had withstood the entire arrest process without a wrinkle.

She was wearing contacts instead of her usual glasses that evening and her medium length straight brown hair was confined by a black velvet bow at the nape of her neck. Her fair face, in spite of the evening's strain, was as appealing as ever to Augie, if not more so in her distress and vulnerability.

She sat listlessly on the loveseat facing the window with the view of the city and accepted a cigarette from Augie. She looked at him with a wan smile. "Thank you for coming to get me, Augie. Funny how with all my friends and acquaintances, even family members here in town, I thought to call you."

"I think that means we're best friends," he told her fondly.

"Oh, Augie, what am I going to do? My whole life is going to be one huge mess because of this."

"Prudence, don't worry. First of all, for a first offense and an insignificant amount, they won't keep your car. They only do that to drug dealers. Secondly, your community service will be a piece of cake, probably counseling at a trauma center. Thirdly, you live close enough to your office to jump on a bus or take a cab without being terribly inconvenienced. Fourthly, drugs are occupational hazards for physicians and this will be taken into consideration before your sentencing. Finally, I have a very good lawyer for your use. So, you see? There's nothing to worry about. You're certainly not going to jail."

"Strange that you're talking sense to me for a change."

"Isn't it?"

"I suppose our professional relationship is now at an end," she reflected, looking at him steadily.

"Ours? Why so?"

"How could you possibly respect my judgment after the events of this evening?"

"Worrying about me on top of everything else?" Augie smiled. "I think you need to take something and get to sleep."

"No! I have to stop taking things. That's what got me into trouble tonight."

"Very well then, drink a nice glass of milk and pull the covers over your head and I'm sure things will look brighter in the morning," he assured her kindly.

When she only brooded in reply he put his arm around her and gave her a hug. "Now promise you'll stop sulking and go straight to bed or I'll have to spank you," he threatened mildly.

She wrapped her arms around his slim torso and clung to him, suddenly quite overwhelmed by his concern. "I deserve to be spanked for my idiotic behavior tonight," she murmured against his chest.

"I'd do it in a heartbeat if I thought it would make you feel better," he told her, hugging her a little harder now and pressing his lips to her cheek.

"You know," she said thoughtfully, "I think it might."

Augie studied her face for a moment and saw shyness, curiosity, and above all, an eagerness to blot out her disgraceful night's work.

"It might hurt," he warned her, shrugging off his jacket and tossing it aside.

"Probably it should hurt," she replied, unconsciously speaking Augie's language.

"Very well then," he sighed, taking the small, slender girl by the waist and gently pulling her across his lap. The little gasp she gave as she went over contracted his heart with pleasure. He had tried many times to imagine Prudence Carr in this position, but the image he had conjured had never approached this degree of adorability. He hadn't realized how neatly firm and rounded she was until that moment. In fact, her bottom was quite perfect.

"Prudence, dear, I'm going to have to lift your little skirt to do this properly," he advised her. She held her breath as he pushed it up to her waist and ran his hand across her black lace Christian Dior panties. She was also wearing garters, seamed stockings and high-heeled ankle-strap shoes that set her nice legs off to advantage. "Why have I never seen you dressed like this before?" he wondered, stroking and squeezing her full, jutting cheeks through the lace briefs.

Prudence didn't answer but did smile at last; the Sheriff's station suddenly a million miles away. Then his hand came down for the first time on her bottom, with a crisp report. This startled an "Oh!" out of her, but wasn't terribly painful. It did sting, but Prudence was certain it didn't hurt, which rather confused her until the next smack fell, causing exactly the same sensation.

Augie gripped Prudence firmly about the waist and began to spank her in a no-nonsense manner. He wasn't really angry at being gotten out of bed in the middle of the night, but he imagined that he was for a couple of moments, in order to work up the correct degree of enthusiasm for disciplining this beautiful young lady, with whom he suddenly realized he was terribly in love.

Prudence couldn't help but sense Augie's gravity as he brought his palm down rapidly but rhythmically on either cheek, and in a way inexplicable to herself, this aroused her. Besides that, though it felt very erotic, it didn't really hurt. To Prudence's amazement, she felt herself beginning to arch to his hand, hoping he would understand that it was perfectly all right to pull her panties down. The full, warm sensation that flooded her entire inner core had nothing to do with pain. Was it possible, Prudence wondered, that she was naturally submissive? Or was it her newly sprung love for Augie that made her so responsive?

"Augie?" Prudence suddenly turned to look over her shoulder at him, "Aren't you going to scold me?"

Augie slowly rolled her panties down to mid-thigh to reveal a white and pink bottom. Smack! "You have been a very bad girl." Smack! Smack! "Partying is one thing, everyone has to let off steam now and then; but speeding through the night directly afterwards wasn't smart. Did you think your car was invisible to radar?"

"I never considered it."

"Young lady, you're getting a hundred of the best, during which I want you to think about how childish you've been tonight." Then he began to bring his hand down in a slow, measured manner, spanking her hard each time it connected with her rosy bottom. "Are you thinking about all the trouble you've caused me tonight?" he asked on stroke twenty.

"Yes, sir," she replied, still unwilling to break the spell of the spanking, though indeed, her bottom was beginning to feel very warm and the sting had increased as well. But instead she thought about how kind and strong he was. It wasn't difficult to suddenly idolize Augie given the spectacular rescue and now, the strangely ticklish feeling produced by the spanking.

Augie went on spanking her and counting in his head towards one hundred, quite amazed at her reaction to the treatment. "I ought to do this more often," he told her, pausing to rub on stroke fifty. In doing so, he pulled off her panties and divided her thighs. She parted them even further, inviting him to touch her. "Why, Prudence, you're sopping wet!" he told her.

"I am? I didn't realize."

"You know, a girl only goes to a party dressed in stockings and a garter belt for one reason," he observed, rubbing the sting away and then delicately spreading her slick labia with his long fingers.

"Oh?" she gasped. "And what is that?"

"To be had, of course," he replied, smacking her hard. "Now you tell me the truth, young lady, was it the decadent doctor who had you that gave you the coke?"

"How did you know he was a doctor? And how do you know he had me?"

"Never mind that. I know you!" The next ten swats came hard and fast. They made her cry out, but still she had no impulse to stop him. "I just want to know why you never dress like this for our sessions."

"Because that might distract you from your problems."

"Well, isn't that the whole idea behind therapy?"

"No. It's to resolve them."

"Well, anyway, I want you to dress like this for me from now on."

"You can't tell me how to dress for our sessions."

"Yes, I can. In fact, I can even change the nature of the therapy if I want to. I can change it to: Stress relief through spanking Dr. Carr."

Prudence either sobbed or laughed. But when he renewed his grip on her waist to administer the final forty, she paid strict attention. Augie noticed that she kept her smooth white thighs parted without being told to do so. The longer and harder he spanked her, the more pliant she became. He believed she could have taken another hundred swats after the first, but could postpone the pleasure of possessing her no longer.

"Ever been had by two different men in one night, Dr. Carr?" Augie asked, bending her over the edge of the bed and pulling her up against him as he quickly unzipped and hauled out the engine of his own pleasure.

"If I answer truthfully I might get another spanking, so I'll say no," Prudence replied, arching prettily for him and inviting him to penetrate her fully.

"You'll get another spanking anyway. First thing in the morning, for all the bother you've put me to tonight," he promised, driving into her snug depths for the first time. "And you know how cranky I can be in the morning."

A little later she cuddled against him in the pre-dawn darkness of her bedroom, naturally tired now from her evening of anxiety and sensations.

"You're canceling your appointments and staying home tomorrow," he told her firmly.

"I'll have to go to the impound lot first thing and pick up my car."

"I'll take care of that for you. I want you to rest all morning," Augie ordered, feeling a lively interest in everything that concerned her now.

"You will?"

"Of course, dear."

"Oh, Augie, I think you really like me," Prudence murmured sleepily. "I only wish you hadn't declared yourself to Teresa yesterday!"

"I didn't do any such thing," he replied, surprised to be reminded of the impulse he'd suppressed.

"You didn't?" Prudence sat up in bed and looked at him with excitement.

"You advised me not to," Augie replied, pulling her back into his arms.

Chapter Four

Pamela

"I've hired an eccentric girl to look after the shop while Laura and I are in Europe," Hugo Sands told Sloan Taylor while browsing in the bookstore. "She's in the scene," the publisher of The New Rod Quarterly added confidentially.

It had been five months since Frankie's dramatic departure and Sloan's social life had been quiet. "She's very retro," Hugo continued. "Lives in a world of her own. I thought you two would get along fairly well. Don't hope for much at first, though. She's difficult."

"And you're trusting her with the shop?"

"Well, she's never actually had a job before, but she's loaded with art school and fashion degrees. I'd have hired her on the outfit she interviewed in alone."

"What did you mean about her being difficult?"

"You'll see."

"Should I behave as though I know she's in the scene?"

"No, don't do that. She considers the scene coarse. She once ran a personal ad and the replies offended her."

"I see."

"You should spank her, of course. She needs someone to. Just don't admit that you're into it. Pretend it's an onerous task."

Hugo picked out a few books for his trip. "Oh, and I hope you don't mind, Sloan, but I told her that if she has any crises at the shop she should seek your counsel."

"It will be my pleasure," Sloan replied sincerely, knowing that Hugo would never have bothered to explain all of this to him unless the girl was very interesting.

Sloan guessed Pamela Crane was Hugo's new clerk the moment she walked into the bookshop the following Monday at noon, a leggy, 25 year old brunette with a high, chestnut brown ponytail and the disdainful, red-lipped pout of fashion Barbie, 1958. She was wearing a black pencil skirt with a French gray peplum jacket and carried a gray umbrella. As she browsed through the classics section Sloan noticed her examining the tips of her lighter gray gloves now and then for specks of dust. She spent fifteen minutes browsing then finally came to the center counter where he sat.

"I'll take these, please," she said, barely looking at him as she dug a tiny purse out of a small handbag. Sloan was impressed by her selections.

"You have exquisite taste," he told her, examining the books by Aphra Behn, Lord Rochester and Voltaire. Pamela stared at him briefly. Then her face became an impassive mask, acknowledging his compliment with the world's faintest smile. She unfolded some bills and waited for her change, checking her watch. Sloan was surprised by her unfriendliness.

Finally receiving her change and package, Pamela clicked out of the store on her dizzyingly high, black, stacked heels. Her long, shapely legs in sheer, seamed black hose and those remarkable shoes were well worth following all the way out the door with one's eyes.

Sloan put up the "Back Later" sign and stalked over to The Puzzle Club for lunch. He was slightly taken aback to find Pamela was already seated with a chicken salad sandwich and a chocolate shake in front of her.

Sloan decided to ignore her and began to immediately work a crossword puzzle, which was printed on the paper tablecloth until his favorite waitress came to take his order. As Sloan flirted with Terry, Pamela's head went up, beguiled by the euphonious sound of his voice. But when she saw it was only the clerk from the bookstore, she dropped her gaze abruptly.

"She can't even spare me a smile," Sloan observed, deciding that this arrogant girl was beginning to get under his skin.

That afternoon brought a mighty thunderstorm to Random Point. Pamela was alone in Hugo's shop when it began and ran to close the upstairs windows.

She had been feeling rather lonely and thunderstorms frightened her. Then, in the midst of the crashing lightning and rolling thunder, a fuse blew and the lights went out all over the shop.

Sloan, who was watching the cobble stoned street fill with thick sheets of rain, noticed the lights go out in Hugo's shop and grabbed his umbrella.

Putting up a sign, Sloan ran across the street to the antiques shop and opened the door calling, "Miss Crane?"

"Hello?" Her voice came from the third gallery above.

"It's me, Sloan, from the bookshop."

"Oh! Thank goodness. It's dark up here and the stairs are very steep!" she complained anxiously.

"Just stay where you are for a minute, and I'll go and hit the breakers," he reassured her, picking his way cautiously through the narrow aisles that led to the back of the shop. Finding the utility room and restoring the power was the work of an instant. As soon as the lights came back on Pamela ran downstairs. They met at the back counter.

"Thank you very much, Mr.?"

"Sloan Taylor. We met earlier at the bookshop today."

"Oh, yes," she looked embarrassed as she reflected on her cool treatment of him that noon. "But what made you come in just then?"

"I couldn't help but notice that your lights went out. And Hugo did ask me to help keep an eye on things while he was away."

"Oh. I see."

"Didn't he mention that to you?"

"Yes, I guess he did," she replied, trembling as another enormous thunder clap rattled the windows in the old wooden building. Sloan, who felt most alive during a thunderstorm, wished this one would end soon for Pamela's sake. "Well, thank you very much for coming over," she said.

"You're welcome. Any time. Perhaps we could have lunch together some day?"

"Thank you, but I always read during lunch," she said, in a slightly apologetic tone, to mitigate the rejection.

"Well, I approve of that," he smiled, in spite of his disappointment. "I'll be going then."

"Good-bye."

Sloan returned to the shop without pleasure, hurt by the fact that even after he'd rescued her, she barely even looked at him. Why was the girl so determined to remain aloof?

But Pamela did miss him after he had gone. She had allowed herself to look at him for the instant it took to mark his height and slenderness, the blackness of his hair and the fairness of his complexion, the cut of his well-made clothes and the grace with which he wore them. She knew very well who he was and had already figured out Hugo's plan to unite them. But Sloan was only a bookstore manager, and falling in love with a poor man was not Pamela's goal.

By day three in Random Point, however, she was becoming very lonely indeed.

Because of her apparent reserve and the limited amount of time he had to make arrangements before leaving for Europe, Hugo hadn't troubled to alert his usual co-conspirators to the new girl's arrival. Since Pamela entertained the naive desire of encountering people in the scene spontaneously, the sophisticated publisher-antiques dealer had decided to let her discover the hidden gems of Random Point for herself or not at all; except for Sloan, with whom he'd become great friends. He envisioned Sloan being her mainstay in the village from the start.

Pamela passed the time when she wasn't in the shop with walks in the woods and on the beach and frequent trips to the vintage video shop to rent very old movies. Sloan's routes were remarkably similar to Pamela's.

She handled the encounter on the beach rather well. She was in a pale dress and straw hat, painting a watercolor and knew very well how enchanting she looked. Sloan only stopped to chat for three minutes, politely discussing the weather. Her heart pounded as she watched him walk away.

The meeting in the woods almost made her dizzy with dread. If there was anything she did not dare let herself do, it was walk in the woods with Sloan. She spotted him, nodded, then walked off the path at a speed which was practically running to avoid any additional contact. She finally did break into a run and did not stop running until the woods opened onto the beach.

Sloan began to lose heart after the incident in the woods, amazed that the mere sight of him could inspire so much distrust. He had never caused such a reaction before and wondered whether Pamela was indeed too odd to pursue.

And yet it made no sense to him that with so much in common, they should both be alone. He refused to believe that she disliked him. She didn't know him well enough to either like or dislike him. But something was causing her to want to keep a distance between them and he didn't think it was another man.

The meeting at the video store went a little better. He knew better than to admire her selection, but he did notice that she had chosen The Girl From Missouri. Luck led them to the checkout counter together and the clerk was on the phone several minutes before attending to them.

"I love this one," he said of her selection. "Do you know this?" He showed her The Palm Beach Story.

"I don't believe I've ever seen it," she admitted in a rush, in spite of her resolve not to converse with Sloan Taylor on any topic of importance.

Now the clerk was off the phone and ringing them up. "Well, good-bye," said Pamela, exiting the store in her usual hurry. Sloan grabbed his video the moment he could and caught up with her.

"Oh, Miss Crane," he fell into step beside the immediately flustered girl, who was in white, high-heeled, ankle strap sandals, white pedal pushers and a sleeveless, red and white checked halter top that knotted above her very slender midriff. A red ribbon pulled back her thick, high, ponytail and she carried a white leather satchel for her videos.

"You startled me," she cried.

"Miss Crane, I was just thinking, you've rented a movie I'd love to see again and I've got one you really ought to see. Why don't we watch our movies together?"

"Thanks, but I don't think so," she replied with great difficulty, however, for she was very lonely and he looked very nice.

"But Miss Crane, here we two are, working in shops on the very same street, dealing with the same clientele, eating at the same restaurants, sharing the same taste in books and movies, and yet we're both alone. Does this make sense to you?"

"I've never thought about it," she replied hesitantly.

"You must have thought about it a little, Miss Crane, or else you wouldn't be so determined to avoid me whenever you can," Sloan declared, finally allowing a hint of irritation to creep into his voice.

"Look, you're extremely attractive, but I just don't have time for a...a romance," she suddenly stated, feeling her face go red.

"Well, who said anything about that?" Sloan quickly replied, "I only meant that now and then we could keep each other company. Particularly as we seem to enjoy so many of the same amusements."

"Oh, come on, it could never be just that with someone like you!" she accused.

"What do you mean, someone like me?" Sloan's surprise was genuine.

"Someone so obviously at least partially Italian!" she informed him decisively.

"Why, how did you know I was partially Italian?" Sloan was immediately charmed and forgave her everything. So she had been looking at him!

"Nose, hair, eyes and the look in them," she replied promptly. They walked past the bookshop and on through the village.

"Yes," he confided, "my mother met my father in Rome, had an embarrassing fling and came home pregnant with me."

"My, you really are Italian," she smiled at her own acumen. He had never seen her really smile before and it changed everything about her. Now they began walking out of the village on Shadow Lane, the narrow, tree-lined road that led to Hugo Sands' house.

"Have you noticed that I'm walking you home?" he asked, relieving her of the leather satchel.

"I don't think you ought to," she argued, though not very persuasively. Suddenly a clap of thunder rent the muggy, Indian Summer sky. "Oh, no!" she cried. "How many thunderstorms must we endure in one week?" She did not attempt to dissuade him from accompanying her home any longer.

It was a half mile walk to Hugo's house, where she was cat sitting for the next three months. She had enjoyed the house, luxuriating in the heaps of esoteric erotica which filled the library and masturbating every a day as a result of being around it.

But even this was no substitute for fine human companionship and Pamela began to realize that she ought to at least try to be friends with the young man and hope for the best. Unfortunately she already found her pulse accelerating whenever she looked at him. And this did not bode well for a young lady who planned to remain unattached.

Pamela's heels were too high for running, so they both became thoroughly soaked before reaching Hugo's house. Once there, she led him upstairs to Hugo's room so that he could borrow some dry clothes. Mounting the stairs behind her Sloan couldn't fail to stare at the perfect proportions of her oval cheeks, which were revealed by her wet pedal pushers.

Pamela had changed into a blue madras sundress and pumps. Her damp hair was now loose and hung to the middle of her back, confined only by a blue grosgrain headband. Sloan was dazzled by the fairy tale whiteness of her skin, redness of her mouth and blackness of her hair and wanted to kiss her. Instead he followed her into the den to watch her movie.

Sloan regretted that neither of their film choices included a spanking scene, as he could well imagine with what rapt attention she would view it, and how vulnerable to seduction she would be directly afterwards.

"This was a good idea," she told him, grinding pepper over the eggs that Sloan had scrambled for her. "I love watching old movies more than almost anything else, but I've never had anyone to talk about them with."

Sloan put his chin on his hand and watched her eat with deep contentment.

"Want to watch the other one as well?" he asked.

"Oh yes, let's!" she clapped her hands, forgetting to be aloof.

As Pamela sat cheering the two films' charming, scheming, fortune hunting heroines, it stuck Sloan like a brainwave: Pamela was one of those girls who planned to capture a wealthy husband!

He considered this revelation as he walked home in the rain under one of Hugo's umbrellas. They had spent many hours together and had talked extensively about art, film and literature, convincing him beyond any doubt that she was ideally suited to be his mate.

And yet she appeared to lack ambition. She told him that she hoped this would be her last job, though she did not expect to distinguish herself at it. She only wished to be remembered as the striking girl in the antiques shop that autumn.

She revealed that she had been sorry to learn that Hugo Sands was encumbered with a lover. He would have been a perfect choice of partner, with his wealth, influence and exquisite taste.

"I don't suppose it even matters if her quarry is in the scene or not," Sloan conjectured aloud, for he was alone on the lane, "so long as he's a marriage-minded millionaire." He splashed though puddles, getting his feet soaked all over again. "Idiotic girl!"

Sloan let Pamela alone for a few days, just long enough to make her tense, then called her at mid-week to ask her to join him for lunch. She agreed and he had her up to his studio above the shop on Wednesday afternoon for a home cooked meal that he'd prepared the night before.

Pamela reflected upon what an excellent husband he would make and told him so. He flushed with pleasure, but protested, "Oh no, I'd make a terrible husband. I'm a perfectionist and a tyrant. "

"You're being too severe on yourself. If I were married to a marvelous man, I'd thank him for taking the time to make everything perfect."

"But I haven't told you everything."

"What's the rest, then?"

"Wives can be so irritating," Sloan mused.

"Well, yes, I suppose they can," Pamela's smile boded mischief for her future husband.

"Do you know what my response would be to a wife or even a dear girlfriend who was irritating me?"

"No, what?"

"Well, I'm sure I'd turn her over my knee."

As Sloan served the Shepherd's pie he was gratified to note a spot of pink appear on each of Pamela's cheeks.

"That wouldn't be such a terrible thing," she replied, peeking briefly at him.

"No? You don't think so? Most women wouldn't agree."

"Well, Sloan, you know I'm a little old fashioned."

Now they ate in shy silence, each wondering about the other. He felt that she now seemed interested in him, almost to the point of melting.

She, far beyond melting and all the way to planning, wondered if she dared use him, just for the night. Surrounded by all the rare erotica, with this handsome boy so close at hand, one more night in Random Point without having sex did not seem possible, even to a young woman as focused and restrained as Pamela. And now there was his mention of spanking!

The lunch hour passed all too quickly and they both returned to their posts behind their respective cash registers. As usual, the bookshop was busy, while the antiques shop welcomed less than two browsers in an hour.

Pamela was to discover, to her amazement, that sales were even more rare. She wondered how Hugo could afford to employ her. But Sloan explained that Hugo did most of his business with private collectors and urged her not to fret about the sales. But she did worry, because it was in her nature to do so. And even though she fully expected to be dismissed at the end of November, when Hugo returned, she made an effort to familiarize herself with the stock, in case any serious customers should happen to ask her a question.

Pamela was re-reading the catalog when her first real buyer walked in. Sloan happened to be at his window when Randy Price entered the antiques shop. The moment before Randy decided to enter, Pamela had been out sweeping the sidewalk, dressed in a cherry red halter sundress, with ankle strap sandals and toenails to match. Today she had worn her hair up and looked as elegant as a runway model, with her glorious cheekbones and wide red mouth.

"Not Randy Price," Sloan muttered to himself. When Randy didn't emerge for over a half hour, Sloan thought, "Well, she's got her millionaire."

Pamela thought so too, and was so excited by the prospect that she ran across the street to tell Sloan as he was locking the door at six.

"Sloan, guess what happened today?"

"You sold something big?"

"How did you know?" she wondered.

"I saw Randy Price go in. What did he buy?"

"That darling bottle green velvet fainting couch. He said he wanted a present for his sister, something elegant but solid, so I showed him the couch. He bought it without even blinking, Sloan, a $2,200 piece! Of which I will receive 5% commission. Isn't it wonderful?"

"I suppose you've got a date?'

"Do you know everything?"

"What I don't know I can sometimes figure out," he replied cynically.

"What's the matter, Sloan? You don't sound very happy for me."

"I'm sorry, honey, it's just that Randy is not a very nice man."

"But, he seemed very nice to me. Isn't he terribly rich?"

"Terribly is the word. He's a land developer of the conscienceless variety. To give you an example, last year he attempted to turn the Random Point duck pond into a strip mall. Fortunately, since it's been on the same site since the 1700's, the township was able to get it declared a national monument in time to stop him."

"Oh," she frowned. "Well, anyway, I got my first sale." The disagreeableness of Sloan's disclosure deflated her and Pamela arrived home anguished at the thought of the potentially displaced ducks.

By the time she was ready to dress for her date, however, she thought only of the fun she would have in going out with a rich man for the very first time.

Nor did Randy disappoint her – initially. He took her to the best inn within twenty miles and feted her in a private suite. The champagne was expensive and went to her head quickly. Even so, she couldn't fail to notice that Randy was much more interested in studying the contours of her shape than probing her intellect.

After the dinner had been cleared away, he hastened to seduce her. As a decadent male in his middle thirties who had long associated with sophisticated women, Randy had some skills, and the not very experienced Pamela was momentarily dazzled. The wine helped still the nagging voice inside her mind that said no, as did the knowledge of his enormous power and resources.

Randy was not in the scene, but he was dominant and Pamela was one of his easiest conquests. The act of taking full possession, from first ear nibble to male orgasm took exactly twenty-five minutes. They finished with Pamela on her knees, while Randy ejaculated copiously into her mouth. This was the climax that Randy had envisioned from the moment he had glimpsed her remarkably full red lips and he was not disappointed by its realization.

However, anything but a romantic, once he had achieved his goal, the need to get away from the girl and back to his life was immediate and urgent.

"Mind if I run you back to town, kid?" he asked over one shoulder as he picked up the room phone to access his messages.

"No," she replied, somewhat dazed, then stumbled to her feet and into the bathroom. She felt quite sick, what with the rich inn food, immediate intercourse and sperm chaser, not to mention feeling violently contemptuous of herself. But she rapidly dressed and repaired her make-up, as willing to depart from Randy as he was to free her.

"Here kid, buy yourself a present," said Randy good-naturedly, while shoving a wad of bills into Pamela's purse just before dropping her off.

"Wow," she breathed in astonishment, spreading the ten, strange, new hundred dollar notes onto her dressing room table a few minutes later. "Keeping a conscience quiet isn't cheap."

The next day when she swept the sidewalk in front of the shop, she wore a plain black cotton bodice dress with a square cut neck and three quarter sleeves. This outfit, of Greek or Italian girl in mourning, seemed to send the message to Sloan that she had been humiliated the previous night. As soon as she went into the shop the phone rang.

"Hugo Sands' Antiques, may I help you?"

"It's me," said Sloan, from behind his own cash register.

"Oh, hello," she said distantly.

"Is everything all right?"

"Yes."

"Anything you want to tell me?"

"Certainly not!" Pamela hung up. Then she walked to her window and glared across the street at him. Sloan appeared at his window and looked back at her. She walked back into the shop and spent the morning brooding. Just before lunch he called her to invite her out. She refused and hung up.

"Why are you avoiding me? I thought we were friends," Sloan asked her the moment she locked the shop door at six to go home. She seemed to jump at his voice but then realized that it was only her heart thumping in her chest.

"I'm a black mood today, Sloan and I'd prefer to be alone," she replied, turning away from the shop. He fell into step beside her and began to walk her out of the village.

"Randy was horrible, wasn't he? I told you he would be."

"Sloan, the last thing I need to hear from you are 'I told you so's'!" she cried, stamping her elegant foot now modestly shod in an Italian skimmer.

"Oh, really? Well, I think you could do with a lot more of the same. And while we're on the subject of things that you need, a good spanking goes right at the top of the list!"

"How dare you talk to me like that?"

"You know it's the truth."

They left the village and began to walk down the lane to Hugo's house. Pamela was capable of strolling rather quickly in flats and the walk was accomplished in half the usual time, which still gave them seven or eight minutes to argue. Sloan felt it would do her good to release some emotion for once and was also fed up with waiting for her to realize his potential, so he prodded her the whole way about Randy's crassness and her own weakness and greed.

"I'll bet he never even asked where you'd been to school," Sloan said incisively, for he knew how proud Pamela was of her education. Pamela narrowed her eyes at him. "What did you wear?" Sloan asked,

117

knowing she couldn't resist replying.

"Oh, a heavenly, little, cream chiffon sheath with a silk under slip. I ran it up myself. You haven't seen it," she said without hesitation.

"It sounds divine. I'll bet he couldn't wait to rip it off."

"Look, I agree that Mr. Price is a Philistine. He used me like a prostitute and even paid me afterwards. He shoved his big cock down my throat and-"

"That's enough," Sloan said, aghast.

"Satisfied now?"

"It's all your fault, you know," he told her. "I tried to warn you about Randy, but all you could think about was some fantasy of marrying a millionaire."

"It's not a fantasy and I'm going to do it. It's just not going to be Randy."

"You mean you still haven't learned your lesson?"

"Randy was unworthy of me, I agree. Next time I'll know better," said Pamela, calmly. "Perhaps Mr. Sands will be able to point me in the direction of someone as amiable as he is eligible when he returns."

"Mr. Sands has already pointed you in the direction of someone who is both amiable and eligible," Sloan replied, with growing annoyance.

"You?" Pamela looked at him as she pushed open the door of Hugo's house and preceded Sloan inside.

"Why not me?" he impulsively seized her hand as soon as she had closed the door behind them. "We're remarkably compatible and you know it." But she pulled away and turned her back on him, folding her arms across her high, well-rounded bosom with a pout he could see reflected in the mirror she faced.

"No. You're poor. You're only a bookstore manager. You have no prospects, no ambition."

"Now see here," he turned her around. "what do you know of my prospects or ambitions? Have you ever asked me about them? Have you ever asked me anything about myself?"

"I'm afraid I'm not really interested," she replied loftily, turning from him again.

"Well you're about to become interested," he declared, taking her in his arms and kissing her long and hard.

"Now you're gonna get it," he told her at length, grabbing her by her forearm and sitting down on the large wooden settle that filled one wall of the foyer, to pull her across his lap. Her full-skirted cotton dress draped beautifully over her oval buttocks and long legs, and Sloan thrilled to the feel of her across his lap at last.

"Sloan, let me go!" she struggled to break the grip he had taken on her slim waist.

"Not until I've proven to you just how compatible we are," he promised, holding her in place with some difficulty, then smacking her sharply, six or eight times. The slaps, landing on alternate cheeks through the skirt, seemed to calm rather than agitate Pamela and her struggling ceased in her realization that he was perfectly serious about giving her a spanking. He heard her catch her breath in excitement and noticed that she made no further move to get away. Encouraged, he spanked her again, harder and faster. She gave a little whimper each time his hand came down but still lay passively across his lap, in ecstasy as she received her first spanking.

"So you can behave when you want to," Sloan reflected, slowly folding her skirt back to her waist. She gave a little pant as he examined her. Her briefs of lavishly embroidered black lace clung to her milky cheeks. She was so lithe that his arm tucked comfortably around her waist and allowed him to virtually cup her sex in his hand while he spanked her.

"I'm sure you never got as wet as you are at this moment the whole time you were with Randy Price," Sloan observed.

"You're unkind to keep taunting me with my mistake," she cried, "and please don't mention that man's name to me again!"

A few more solid smacks and he could see the pinkness clearly through the lace.

"By the way," he delivered several more hard smacks, "I never want to hear you use such language again as you did to describe your adventures with Randy."

"Very well," she murmured, so enjoying the feel his palm pressed against her sex through her panties.

"As you normally speak like such a lady, I was doubly shocked," he went on, pausing to rub her between harder smacks that he made her wait for one by one.

"You wouldn't expect to use me like that, would you, Sloan?" she turned to look at him.

"I don't expect to use you at all," he smiled, but gently pushed her head back down. "I expect to take you in hand, young lady."

"But, what does that mean?" she reached back to rub her bottom but he pushed her hand away and finally removed his own from between her satiny thighs.

"It means that it's time for these panties to come down," he said, tugging them slowly down over her cheeks and to mid-thigh. "Oh, Pamela," he breathed, lightly kissing her exposed flesh, "you should see the pink against the cream. I'll send you a bouquet of the exact colors tomorrow, so you can appreciate it too."

She waited quietly as he tightened his grip on her waist and began to spank her again. "There's a lot you have to answer for," he reminded her, between hard smacks. "Your initial unfriendliness, for example." Six spanks followed. "Then there's this fortune hunting fantasy you seem so determined to act out. Don't you realize how anachronistic your behavior is?" Several dozen hard wallops followed this observation, finally inspiring wriggles and kicks.

"Ow! Why is it? I'm young, attractive, well educated, properly packaged. Why can't I enjoy a life of ease and luxury?" she protested.

"I'm sure you can, but you still ought to be punished for being a shallow, materialistic, misguided, delusional, brat!"

"Am I really all those things?" she wondered to herself as subsequent smacks fell. She didn't think she was shallow, but supposed she might seem that way to Sloan. As to materialistic, wasn't everyone? It was true that she had been misguided with regard to Randy, and as Sloan had attempted to warn her, she was shamed by this insult most of all. Delusional? She disagreed. Of course she knew that her goals were not going to be accomplished as easily as in a movie, but given the proper exposure, she hoped to be discovered like a treasure some time soon.

"It must be terribly embarrassing to be treated like this by a lowly clerk," he snapped, "Too bad you can't have me fired." Smack!

Smack! Smack! "You could always complain to Mr. Sands, but I doubt you'd get much sympathy. He was the one who told me you'd be difficult."

"He did?" she twisted on his lap.

"Since I'm taking the time to discipline you," he pressed her back down, "you will please do me the courtesy of holding your position and not causing me extra trouble," Sloan said sternly, sending a perfect tidal wave of excitement through her flat, little tummy.

"Is it a trouble?" she couldn't help turning again.

"Spanking a girl who isn't the slightest bit interested in one can only be considered a duty."

"Oh, really! Well, you needn't bother, I'm sure!" cried Pamela, trying to cover her bottom with her hand. Sloan caught her gracefully manicured hand by the wrist and slapped it sharply before letting it go. The skin on her delicate hand was so thin that the tap was a good deal more painful than Sloan intended for it to be and suddenly triggered a torrent of sobs and tears from the overwrought young lady.

Once she began to sob he stopped spanking her and pulled her up to sit beside him on the settle. When he saw that she was crying real tears he pulled her against him in the most satisfying hug she had ever felt. "Why, you baby," he murmured, kissing her brow, "I only tapped your hand." She locked her arms around his waist and inhaled his spicy scent for the first time. Her tears quickly ceased as the pain faded, but she clung to him hard, feeling she could never tire of his arms around her.

"The only way to cleanse me of last night's misadventure is for you to take me yourself," she dared to suggest, raising her eyes to his. He kissed her full lips thoughtfully but then shook his head.

"No."

This statement surprised them both and they stared at each other. She then jumped to her feet with an angry blush. She had never in her life been rebuffed before and it particularly stung coming from Sloan. Fresh tears sprang to her eyes and spilled onto her face. Regretful but not moved beyond reason, he reached for her hand and kissed it.

"I'm sorry," he explained. "But I don't want to be used for sex anymore than you do. And since I'm apparently not good enough to

121

have a relationship with, that's all you'd be doing. So, no thank you."

Pamela looked at him with glistening eyes as he walked to the door. "Are you going so soon?" she asked, quite amazed at how unhappy this thought made her.

"I don't think it would be safe to stay any longer," he told her stiffly and marched out.

After he was gone Pamela tried to figure out where she currently stood with Sloan and couldn't decide whether he liked or detested her. The last thing she expected him to do was refuse her favors. After what had happened with Randy, it seemed rather ludicrous to withhold from someone she passionately admired what she had given so freely to another whom she didn't even like.

But Sloan apparently chose to be offended by her sincere offer. And it was sincere too. After he left she was as restless as a cat. She'd fantasized about spanking all her life, but had never imagined how deliriously sexy a real spanking could feel. The way Sloan spanked, it was easy to imagine that Leslie Howard or Melvin Douglas was doing the job. What a charming man he was!

Sloan was not normally an unkind person, but circumstances played out in such a way over the following week that he was able to punish Pamela for all the slights she had inflicted upon him in classic style. It happened that young Susan Ross was due to arrive in Random Point for a ten day holiday before beginning the fall semester at design school, while her lover, Anthony Newton, was not to join her for at least five days. Susan, who was Pamela's 22 year old, small, blonde counterpart, without the neuroses and with the millionaire already in tow, was extremely fond of Sloan and had been planning for about six months to find a way to become better friends with the book seller. The calendar was now in Susan's favor and she intended to make the most of her opportunity.

Sloan introduced the girls on Susan's first night in the village. They all had drinks together at the inn and Pamela was stricken to observe the easy camaraderie that existed between Susan and Sloan.

Sloan had apprised Susan of the strange situation prevalent between himself and Pamela and his friend from New York understood her role. It did not contrast with the one she'd devised for herself. Naturally she wanted Sloan to have Pamela and was perfectly willing to make the silly girl jealous if it would help his cause.

After finishing two glasses of wine with Susan and Sloan, Pamela was anything but eager to leave them and return to Hugo's solitary house, but there seemed to be no graceful way of remaining with the two who had already arranged to spend the evening together.

Walking back to Hugo's house alone in the dusk, Pamela felt profoundly uneasy without knowing why. By the next afternoon, however, when she spotted Susan Ross strolling into the bookshop to pick up Sloan for a luncheon date, Pamela knew why the sight of Susan and Sloan together filled her chest with tightness and her heart with despair.

The torture continued for several days. Because of her shop's proximity to the bookshop, that store's entrance was constantly before her eyes and every time Susan entered or exited it, Pamela noticed. Having no other friends in Random Point exacerbated the situation and by mid-week, crying herself to sleep had become as much of a routine as brushing her teeth. She could only imagine how perfectly the small-sized Susan fit across Sloan's knee and did so until she felt ill.

Neglected and undervalued by Pamela, Sloan gave himself up to Susan's praiseful attentions with voluptuous abandon. They played every night and upon Susan's urging, Sloan ignored Pamela for several days, during which the willowy brunette virtually stopped eating. When Sloan finally ran into Pamela on Thursday afternoon at the bank he was shocked to note how thin she had become and waited for her on the street when she came out.

"Pamela, what's going on? Are you all right?" They began walking back down Shadow Lane towards their shops.

"Why? Don't I look okay?" she demanded, glancing in a store window they passed.

"No, you look awful."

"Me?" She looked at him in surprise.

"You're skin and bones. Haven't you been eating lately?"

"I guess my appetite has fallen off a bit lately," she admitted quietly.

"Well, you've got to force yourself," he told her with concern.

Twenty minutes after Pamela returned to the antiques shop Sloan strolled in with a casserole. "Hi, dear," he said, on his way to the back of the shop. "I'm going to pop something in the oven for you."

"Thanks," she said with a faint smile.

"Promise you'll eat?" he asked, emerging from the kitchenette.

"Yes."

"Good. I have to get back to the shop now."

"Sloan?"

"Yes?"

"I haven't seen you in days."

Sloan flushed and his heart began to pound as he heard her voice break. "If you missed me you ought to have come over to visit," he pointed out.

"I haven't felt wanted lately," she suddenly declared.

"I'm sorry."

"You don't seem to have time for anyone but that little blonde flirt!" said Pamela vehemently. Sloan looked at her in great surprise. Her jealousy was encouraging and flattering, but the insult to Susan displeased him.

"That little blonde flirt happens to be a warm, real human being," Sloan replied briefly, for he could tell she was stretched to the limit and about to snap. "However, this is neither the time nor the place for such a discussion. I have to get back to my shop," he murmured and disappeared into the street.

Pamela took a measure of comfort in the casserole, the visit, even the scolding. But when she looked out the window at six and saw Susan coming to call for Sloan yet again, despair overwhelmed her. She could not remember ever feeling so miserable in her life. Staying home alone was doing her no good but she didn't know where to go to lose herself. Finally she decided on the Bone and Feather Inn pub.

When she discovered that Susan and Sloan were already in a booth, Pamela considered walking out, but as they had already spotted her, she only waved and took a seat at the bar. She might pretend she was waiting for someone if they asked. Before she ordered a drink, Sloan appeared at her elbow. "Pamela, join us!"

"Uh, no, I don't think I will. I'm just having a quick drink then heading home," she replied, unable to meet his eyes.

"Please stay and have dinner with us," he asked as sweetly as he knew how, for he had just been confiding to Susan the terrible state he had found Pamela in that afternoon and they had been deciding what to do about it.

"No, thanks, three's a crowd," she told him bravely, turning to give Connie her order.

"In that case, I see someone who can join us," Sloan declared with satisfaction as former Lt. Michael Flagg, late of the Random Point police department, strode into the room with the relaxed air of a man who had just gone fishing. Sloan met him at the entrance, quickly explained their need for a fourth at their booth and in a minute Pamela's difficulty was resolved. She found herself seated next to Susan and across from the new man, a thirty-something-ish Celtic god in khaki trousers and a blue chambray shirt.

"Enjoying the civilian lifestyle?" Susan asked the recently retired, 6'3" detective with whom she had enjoyed a passionate little affair the previous year.

"More than I thought possible," he replied, giving Pamela an interested once over. "Are you just visiting Random Point or have you moved here?" he asked.

"I'm taking care of Hugo Sands' shop for the autumn."

"And where did Hugo find you?"

"Oh, we just knew each other," replied Pamela vaguely, for the last thing she intended to admit to the stranger was that she subscribed to Hugo's magazine. Michael looked at Susan and raised his eyebrows in a question, to which Susan replied with a nod but then pressed a finger to her lips. This Michael interpreted to mean that: Yes, Pamela was one of them, but that he wasn't to allude to it.

"Where's Patricia tonight?" Susan asked casually.

"She's in Boston till tomorrow," Michael replied, "how about Anthony?"

"He's not due in till the day after tomorrow," Susan reported. Pamela watched the two exchange catlike smiles and felt her own heart contract with hope.

"I don't suppose you have any time to get together between now and then?" Michael asked idly.

"I'm free after dinner as far as I know," said Susan promptly, for she was as worried as Sloan about Pamela's decline and thought it time to stop tormenting their new resident beauty.

Dinner was ordered along with several bottles of wine, and Pamela ate properly for the first time in days. The new male was smooth and amusing as he told stories of life on the Boston police force and his recent forays into the murky and poorly paid field of crime fiction writing. Pamela was shy and hardly spoke, preferring to enjoy the thrill of sitting opposite Sloan in respectful silence. Whereas Susan, she noticed, took every opportunity to tease Michael. Finally Flagg said to Sloan, "Has she been this rambunctious all day?" Susan blushed and subsided in the booth, unwilling to be discussed like this in front of Pamela.

"She's just over-excited seeing you again," Sloan explained happily, for it seemed to him the time was finally right to claim Pamela. Meanwhile, after a couple of glasses of wine, Pamela began to relax. Soon she was laughing out loud and contributing to the conversation. Several hours passed quickly in the company of her new friends. And when it was time to leave, Pamela found that she no longer hated Susan Ross.

"Would you like to come back to my place?" Sloan asked her on the street outside the inn, after Michael took Susan away in his car.

"You're asking me to come home with you?"

"I am."

"Because Susan isn't available?" she snapped back, in spite of herself.

"Is that what you think?"

"What should I think after not hearing from you in so many days?"

"You should think about behaving better when we're together," Sloan told her sternly, taking her by the hand and walking her back to the bookshop.

"But, I tried to be nicer to you the last time we were together and you rejected me!" she accused, made indignant by the memory and bold by the wine.

"I simply thought we should wait until you had developed some feeling for me before becoming intimate," he pointed out logically, leading her upstairs.

"And I suppose Susan Ross is positively teeming with feeling for you?"

"I didn't say that."

"But you did spend the last three nights with her."

"Well?"

"Even though she has another lover who will be here in two days."

"That's just it. We may never have this opportunity again."

"I don't understand. This doesn't sound like you. You condone the fact that she's cheating on her lover? You admire a girl who would do that?"

"It's not cheating. It's only playing. You wouldn't understand."

"Well, explain," she urged him as he lit a couple of candles in his sitting room.

"You see, Pamela, some girls would rather be spanked than kissed. Susan is one of them."

"I see!" Pamela observed coolly, inwardly burning with jealousy. "Well, I think it's disgraceful that she has to play, as you call it, with every male on Cape Cod just because her boyfriend happens to be out of town for three minutes."

"At least Susan doesn't sleep with men she doesn't like just because they have money."

"Oh! That was unnecessarily cruel."

"Was it? I never have gotten over how easily you gave yourself to Randy Price."

"Sloan, I do regret that mistake," Pamela lied, for she had great plans for the thousand dollars, including a new sewing machine and the most voluptuous silks, satins and velvets her remaining allowance would buy. "Need you keep reminding me of it?"

"I'm just trying to point out how unfair you're being to little Susan."

"Little Susan, is she? How adorable."

"Pamela, don't try for sarcasm."

"Don't tell me what to do."

"It's time someone did."

"Well, it isn't going to be you."

"I think it will be."

"I still don't understand why it's appropriate for you and Susan to make love without being committed to each other, but it isn't right for you and me," Pamela persisted, getting a cigarette out of her purse. Sloan grabbed a matchbox and lit it for her, then sat down beside her on the divan.

"Susan and I are just friends and always will be. You and I can be something different to each other if you'll only give up this foolish notion of marrying for money and let nature take its course."

"But, why can't you and I just have fun without a commitment?"

"That arrangement might have suited me in the beginning, but it doesn't now," Sloan replied bluntly.

"Well, I can't say I'm surprised to find you so cool," Pamela observed, getting up to take a turn around the room, "after all, you've been gorging on apricot jam for three days!"

Sloan's eyebrows went up and he smiled slightly but didn't reply.

"Look," she flared, "you can't expect me to change my game plan overnight just because I meet a handsome boy."

"Is that how you think of me? As a boy?" Sloan bristled.

"Well," she smiled tenderly, in spite of herself, "you haven't a line anywhere. How old are you, anyway?"

"I'm thirty. Just the right age for you."

"Thirty, are you? I had no idea. That's a very sexy age for a man."

"Now about my prospects. The last time we spoke you seemed to think I had none. I feel you should know that this isn't the case."

"Oh, never mind that comment, I was very rude that day," she protested with some embarrassment.

"All the same, you ought to know that I have a respectable cash inheritance from my mother which will pretty much allow me to make an offer to my employer for the shop. I happen to know that her husband would like her to sell it. It's a nice little business, with purpose and integrity. You could help me with it."

"It's very tempting," she said softly, "but don't think I can afford that particular fantasy."

"I don't understand."

"I need money. Lots of it. And I'm not going to find it in a tiny berg like Random Point."

"Why do you need so much money, Pamela? You eat nothing and make your own clothes."

"Sloan, I've spent the last eight years in the most expensive schools in the country and financed most of it. I owe over a hundred and twenty thousand dollars for my education."

"I see," Sloan replied gently, for this admission revealed that her misguided millionaire-hunting plans had been laid more as a result of desperation than greed.

"Oh, I know what you're going to say, Sloan, why don't I start making use of all my degrees and go get a high powered job, right?"

"You do have everything going for you," said Sloan. "What is it, Pamela, laziness or fear?"

"Both, I suppose," she admitted, leaning her chin on her hand.

"You know, Pamela, I can help you pay off that loan."

"No. I couldn't let you."

"Not even if I were your husband?"

Pamela flushed with pleasure at the proposal.

"You want to marry me?"

"You're the only girl I've ever really wanted to marry."

"But, we haven't even had sex yet. We don't know if it will work."

"Don't be silly, darling, I could make you come with one hand tied behind my back."

"You could?" Pamela grinned.

"Tell me that you love me first," he said, wrapping his arms around her.

"I adore you," she replied, tightening her own arms around his slender torso.

"You know, of course, that nothing can be done until you've had your spanking," he said, pulling her across his lap.

"But, I haven't done anything," she protested softly.

"That's the problem!" Smack! Smack! His hand came down hard on the back of her skirt. "You've got a big debt to pay off young lady, and here you are with a job that pays four hundred dollars a week.

What have you been doing in your spare time?" More spanking. "You should be running up dresses for the nicest shop in town, modeling at the department store, putting canvases in the local art galleries - why I can think of a dozen ways for you to make money in Random Point."

"I'll do what ever you tell me to," she replied helpfully. This got her a rub. Then Sloan sighed, turning back her skirt carefully. This time she was wearing sheer beige panties and her legs were bare. Now she received a sustained spanking over her panties, until the beige turned to rose under his hand. Pamela wriggled and ground against his thighs, but made no effort to break free.

He was charmed by how nicely she took her spanking. Her breathless enjoyment of the position, the scolding, the sharp, stinging smacks, was constantly apparent. He had no idea of what might be going on in her odd little head. Perhaps she was envisioning him a character out of one of her old movies or novels. Whatever she was thinking, her movements, her whimpers, her delirious scent, all conveyed sensual bliss.

"I'm going to marry you," Sloan promised, pulling her panties off, "and keep you right here in Random Point with me. Now what do you think about that?" He let her think while he continued the spanking.

"But you said you're a tyrant," she protested.

"Oh, you have no idea, darling," he promised, daring for the first time to separate her thighs and her bottom cheeks. "Now let me really look at you."

Pamela could not know quite how pretty she looked from that angle, but she had a fair notion that she was being admired as he stroked and examined her.

"Good girl," he told her, delicately peeling open her petals to expose the glistening pinkness within, "I'm relieved that you know when to stop being modest." At this, Pamela arched her bottom slightly and spread her thighs a little wider, to let him see even more of her sex. Sloan inserted one long, middle finger into her wet pussy to the knuckle, causing her to squirm and whimper. "How responsive you are," he pulled his finger free and put it to his tongue to taste her. "But I'm just as interested in understanding this part of you," he said, dividing her bottom cheeks as widely as possible to expose her anus.

"Oh!" she cried, with a blush, but did not try to resist the more intimate examination.

"Lie still," he warned her, slapping her once on each cheek before holding her spread apart, with her tiny, rose-colored bottom hole throbbing and ready to be penetrated. "How do you feel about being touched here?" In so saying, Sloan pressed his palm against her anus.

"I...like it," she replied shyly.

"I suppose you must find it a little embarrassing, though?"

"That's why I like it."

"Perhaps I should save taking you there for our wedding night," Sloan suggested.

"So long as that's the only thing you save for our wedding night," she told him archly.

"Oh?"

"Now that's twice I've asked you to make love to me. I won't do it again," she warned. Sloan turned her around on his lap and took her in his arms.

"I only wanted to wait until you were ready, dear," he murmured, nuzzling her ears and throat. Sloan stood up with Pamela in his arms and bore her into his bedroom.

"Now just lie still and let me undress you," he told her, gently removing her dress, filmy embroidered brassiere, garter belt, stockings and shoes. Pamela was shy but enjoyed his admiration of her slim, tall-girl charms. "You know, you're flawless," he observed, caressing her high, round bosom and flat tummy with sensitive fingertips, then rolling her over to examine every satiny inch of her back, from the nape of her neck to her slim ankles. "But just because you're beautiful, that doesn't mean I'm going to let you get away with things," he warned, smacking her bottom sharply twice, then pulling her up by the hips. "Lean on your hands, dear," he told her, simultaneously spreading her legs and unzipping his trousers.

In a moment he was in her, his hands fastened to her small waist, his cock deeply lodged in her impossibly snug vagina and excitement coursing through every fiber of his body.

"I'm afraid I don't come," she explained after one or two happy minutes of deep, well-lubricated thrusting.

"What, Pamela?" Sloan paused and lightly rocked back and forth inside her while she explained.

"Well, this feels thrilling, but don't expect me to climax."

"In this position, I don't," he agreed, then continued thrusting, but at a slower pace, while at the same time slipping one hand under her tummy to hold her even closer against him. Pamela caught her breath in surprise at how sexy his palm felt pressed just above her Venus Mound. "I just don't climax with partners."

"If you can climax by yourself, you can climax with a partner."

"Not me."

Sloan sighed, grabbed the long bolster at the head of his bed and slipped it under Pamela, so that she straddled it. "Feel different?" he asked.

"Yes!" she replied, immediately aware of her sex pressed against the firm pillow while his cock filled her deeply from behind.

"And the nice thing about this position is that I can spank you while I'm penetrating you," he observed, smacking her hard several times on each cheek, then pulling them apart and smacking her in the middle just as hard. "I can stop to discipline you anytime I like," he told her, going back to thrusting while she caught her breath, then pausing to spank her some more, and so on, back and forth, until Pamela's suddenly awakened clitoris burst into an ecstatic orgasm approximately two minutes later. Her own convulsive spasms causing Sloan's own release to be imminent, he remembered that he had not put a condom on and jerked his penis free in time to shower her pink and white cheeks with his liquid tribute.

Later, as they sat in bed in the moonlight, making their plans, Pamela continued to wonder at his magical ability to wring an orgasm from her the very first time they'd made love when no one else ever had.

"I'm at your service always," he promised. "But when shall we get married? Next week or next month?"

"At Christmas," she decided. "I'll need time to make my dress."

"That's a good idea. Meanwhile, I can try to make those arrangements about the shop with Marguerite."

"Marguerite?"

"Mrs. Branwell, the woman who owns the bookstore. You might as well know that something happened between us fairly recently."

"Something?" Pamela's heart lurched painfully.

"I lost my head one day and pulled her down on my lap. You can figure out what happened next. It was entirely my fault, though she didn't resist. Her husband found out because my ex-girlfriend discovered what had happened and sent him a spiteful note. Malcolm forgave Marguerite almost immediately, but my little Frances went straight back to Boston, telling me to go to hell. She was my assistant in the bookshop. Don't look like that Pamela; I was fond of her, but not in love. She didn't have the sort of character I admire."

"Your character is beginning to look a lot less upright every second," Pamela observed, sitting up in bed. "Are you saying that while you were making love to your employee you were also seducing your boss?"

"Darling, you have to understand, it was an unusual situation."

"Sloan, such duplicity!"

"You see, it was like this -"

"I don't think I want to hear anymore."

"Well, you're going to anyway, because if you don't hear it first from me, you'll soon hear it from someone else and I won't have you draw the wrong conclusions."

"I don't expect to be discussing your sex life with other people any time soon."

"I'm sure you don't, but this is a small community, especially in the winter when the tourists are gone. And friends do talk about friends."

"Very well, I'll listen, but I won't like it," she pouted, lighting a cigarette.

"Oh good!" he said, pulling on a grey bathrobe and sitting in the window seat to avoid her smoke. "Well, Marguerite had this romantic idea of staffing her shop with two people in the scene. So she hired me along with a pretty little Radcliffe girl, who was happy to become my temporary counterpart. Everything was going fairly well -- not perfectly, you understand, but all right, when Frances suddenly caught cold and stayed home from work for eight days. This necessitated Marguerite coming back to work temporarily in the shop and that's when it happened. I realize now that it all turned out for the best."

"How so?"

"Well, Frances wasn't for me. She wasn't sweet tempered, like you."

"You think I am?"

"I do."

"Well, perhaps you're right. I certainly wouldn't run away from you for making one mistake, or even several," Pamela declared fondly.

"You see, I knew you were like that."

"I understand about Italian blood."

"Of course, now that we're engaged, I have no intention of ever looking at another woman," he swore passionately.

"Nor I at another man," she pledged.

"Oh, you will all right," he sighed.

"You'll see."

"Won't I, though," he sighed.

Chapter Five

Phoebe and Pascal Part 1

Pascal Robbins, 36, was a photojournalist who had obtained a contract to shoot scenic Cape Cod for a coffee table book. His wife Phoebe Casper, 26, was an actress who'd signed on with the Woodbridge Repertory Theatre Group for the Autumn season. They were subletting William Random's house in the cul-de-sac at the end of Shadow Lane.

The Robbins were an unusually attractive couple. Pascal was a lithe, angular, sartorially traditional male, who wore trousers with pleats, shoes with laces, and hats. Phoebe had first become aware of him as he stared at her from the sixth row center two consecutive nights while she played Beatrice in Much Ado About Nothing the previous year in Boston.

Phoebe's sprightliness helped her land roles in the comedies of Goldoni and Moliere, her scaled down voluptuousness showing to advantage in period costumes. Her mellifluous voice had seduced him, while her long, burnished hair and lambent eyes, all aglow in the footlights, worked a swift enchantment on Pascal.

The Robbins had been married for less than a year, barely knew each other, were passionately in love and quarreled whenever they met, which wasn't often. It had been a rocket year for Pascal, filled with international travel and spreads in magazines, while Phoebe had spent the hardest winter of her life with a theatre group in Minneapolis, only seeing her new husband for a few days every month.

But now the coincidence of them both finding work in this idyllic location, during the most romantic season of the year, held Phoebe enthralled.

Pascal and Phoebe were well meaning but equivalently difficult people. Both were willful, emotional, defensive, and classically high strung but with many opposing traits. For example, while Pascal was a meticulous planner, Phoebe's methods often seemed as scattered as pick-up sticks.

The first time Pascal saw her turn a hotel suite into a yard sale simply by unpacking, he fancied he could feel his blood pressure rise. Luckily, whisky had the power to calm him, and he availed himself of its beneficial properties whenever he felt himself in danger of losing his temper with his adorable new wife.

Pascal had lived as a fussy bachelor for so long that making the adjustment to co-habitation with a bouncing, cheerful, sun-tea brewing, non-smoking, non-drinking, decaffeinated, exercise conscious, Green Party crusading vegetarian was a tremendous challenge.

Unlike Pascal, Phoebe never suffered from anxiety, slept like a small, mossy stone and never awoke without a pink flush in her face and dazzlingly clear eye whites. All of this thrilled and annoyed him no end and he vacillated between feeling unworthy of her and repressing the urge to wring her smug little neck.

Often, over his first cup of coffee (that he himself ground, since she lacked all domestic skills) and cigarette of the day, he'd watch her flit around the charming old kitchen, leaving messes in her wake, and fantasize about forcing her to behave like a lady.

First he mentally replaced the tee shirt of his that was all that she wore, with a silk dressing gown and high-heeled slippers. Next, instead of yogurt and whole grain bread, he imagined her fixing them eggs Benedict and Mimosa, without spilling or slopping or breaking anything. That was as far as the fantasy went but it always made him sigh with longing.

When Phoebe sat down and dug into her granola while casually turning the pages of The Nation, Pascal noticed how much like the hands of a twelve year old Phoebe's appeared.

"You bite your fingernails?" he took her small hand in his slim, graceful one and shook his head with disapproval.

"It's just a nervous habit," she confessed, hiding her free hand in her lap with a blush.

"You, nervous?"

"I guess I must be, huh?" Now she stopped eating and sat on both hands.

"Ever think of a manicure?"

"You mean put on toxic polish?"

"But crimson nails are so sexy," he replied, picking up The New York Times.

The organic Phoebe snorted in derision but the actress who enjoyed adopting new personae decided to obtain a manicure that afternoon.

That day magic happened for Phoebe Casper Robbins. First, the moment she arrived home, she received the call from the casting director telling her that she had been selected for the role of "Nora" in A Doll's House, the opening play of the season. This news caused Phoebe to perform cartwheels around the back garden.

Within the next half hour, as she wandered around the old house, allowing the thrill of popularity to wash through her, Phoebe made a discovery that relegated even Nora to the back of her mind momentarily. She was in William Random's study when she came across an antique riding crop in the drawer of her landlord's desk.

Phoebe's heart began to pound as she examined it. She hadn't had a spanking fantasy since she had gotten married, but the sight of the crop immediately recalled her secret passion. She wondered what Pascal would say when she showed it to him. Perhaps he'd turn her under his arm and use it on her for snooping!

Being an intuitive young lady, Phoebe was inclined to believe that the crop she held had not been used on a horse in some time. This in mind, she began to look more carefully into the cabinets and drawers, not only of the study, but of other rooms in the house. By the time Pascal got home, Phoebe felt she knew more about the sex life of William Random than she knew about her own.

"I found out some fascinating facts about the people who own this house," Phoebe confided to Pascal the moment he came in around teatime. He kissed her and began to de-camera in the handsome foyer.

"Really? Tell me," he encouraged her as she led him into the sitting room where she actually had the samovar heating. She had the flame turned up so high that the silver bottom had oxidized to black, but he was touched by the gesture. "You can't have this turned up so high, darling, you'll ruin the samovar," he told her gently, turning down the flame and wiping the bottom clean with a napkin.

"I'm sorry, but wait until you hear. Guess what I found in William Random's desk?" She carefully prepared a cup of tea for her husband, using a silver tea ball stuffed with real tea leaves from a tin on the sideboard. This genteel occupation suddenly brought back the real news of the day and she spilled half the tea as she turned in excitement to cry, "I can't believe I forgot, I'm to play Nora!"

"You're to play Nora?" Pascal took her in his arms. "Little you?"

"I'm just as shocked as you are," she confided, breaking from his embrace in order to cram a chocolate covered apricot into her mouth. "You're eating chocolate?" Pascal was amazed.

"I have to start living and breathing Nora. Be prepared for a five pound weight gain in the coming days and weeks," Phoebe was philosophical. "If we start corseting you right away, no one need ever notice," he teased her, pulling her down on his lap.

"I can't believe you mentioned corsets! That's just what I was coming to about the Randoms!"

"Don't tell me William Random corsets to achieve those rock-hard abs?" Pascal protested.

"Silly. His lover, that gorgeous Puerto Rican girl, has a world-class collection of waist cinches in her wardrobe plus leather dresses, stiletto heels and opera gloves for days. I tell you these people are serious fetishists!"

"Mr. Random's Significant Other is a very feminine creature," Pascal observed when Phoebe jumped off his lap to pour herself a cup of tea.

"You like that, don't you?" she accused with sudden excitement.

"You're very feminine, darling," he told her, taking the teacup away and pulling her back down on his lap. She casually regarded her freshly enameled nails until he noticed them. "Phoebe, you followed my advice!" He was overwhelmed and kissed her hands.

"Nora is docile and obedient, always," Phoebe replied, with a serious gaze.

"Except for when she's doing exactly as she pleases," Pascal pointed out, squeezing her small waist.

"Nora trembles when her husband frowns," Phoebe insisted gravely.

"And you intend to follow suit?'

"Just for the next three weeks."

"Oh, I see," he smiled.

"Guess what else I found? Just wait until I show you!" Phoebe ran out of the room and reappeared in the sitting room a minute later, carrying a large, chestnut leather album with peach cherubs carved into the cover. She laid it on the coffee table and sat down next to him.

"Now get ready for some racy stuff," she warned, beginning to turn the black pages, upon which a collection of artistic, black and white photos paraded. Some pictured pretty women in exotic attire, posing in studio settings, while others were of attractive couples in fancy dress at what appeared to be fetish balls. Included were a number of spanking stills and others, which involved more esoteric forms of corporal punishment. In every case, the dress, positioning and expressions were perfect. Phoebe watched Pascal's face closely as he turned the pages with an interest that was real but which fell far short of the fascination they had held for her.

Phoebe had spent some time with the album, returning again and again to the six perfect, over the knee spanking portraits, which appeared in the middle of the book. This pretty collection also caught Pascal's eye and he grinned at her.

"That's what you could use sometimes, a good spanking!"

This comment left her momentarily bereft of speech and she simply stared at him. "Do you really think so, darling?" she finally stammered, blushing hard.

"Just about three or four times a week," he reassured her, pulling her towards him and kissing her. Then he let her go and began to turn the pages of the album again. She wondered that he could go through the beautiful photographs so rapidly.

"I wonder who she is." Pascal mused, as he came to a photo of a brunette who wasn't Damaris perched on William Random's lap.

"Her name is Laura. She's his ex. Come with me!" Phoebe took him by the hand and led him upstairs to William's studio and unlocked the door.

"Phoebe, I don't remember William giving us the key to this room," Pascal said as he followed her inside. As the workspace of an architect, this was one of the most beautiful rooms in the house. But the most interesting aspect of the decor was the gallery of framed illustrations, which decorated the walls.

These drawings, mostly done in colored pencil or gouache and all signed by Laura Random, portrayed even more esoteric forms of bondage and discipline than were displayed in the photo album.

"Phoebe, where did you get the key to this room?" Pascal demanded.

"From William Random's desk," she replied, with a palpable flutter.

"And do you think he would have locked the room if he wanted us in here?"

"I don't know. Does it matter? He'll never know."

"Are you kidding? You can't look at a room without destroying half the objects in it."

"You make me sound like "Carrie"," she observed, not unflattered by his estimation of her powers.

"Come on, baby, give me the key."

"The key? But why do you want it?" Phoebe reluctantly dug the key out of the pocket of her khaki shorts and put it in his hand.

"To make sure you never come in here again. Now let's go," he told her, pulling her out the door and locking it behind them, then putting the key in his own pocket.

"Really, darling, you hardly even looked at the drawings!" Phoebe folded her arms and sulkily followed him downstairs again.

"Sweetheart, the owner left that door locked for a reason and I think we should respect it."

"But I'm sure it was only because they didn't want to shock us."

"Then why leave the photos out?"

"They just forgot about the photos. I know, because I found plenty of other stuff they did lock up!" said Phoebe triumphantly; but her glee evaporated as she noticed his frown.

"Phoebe, that's not nice," he declared, heading for the whiskey as soon as they reentered the sitting room. "We should respect the privacy of others."

"I'm sure they wouldn't mind," she replied intuitively.

"Phoebe, how can you say such a thing?"

"Because men who take photos like those don't get upset when women find them thrilling."

Pascal threw her a sharp look at this declaration. "Nevertheless, I want you to stay out of that studio from now on," he told her, lighting a cigarette.

"But I hadn't nearly finished looking at the beautiful drawings," Phoebe brooded, kicking her tiny work-booted foot against the delicately carved leg of a sofa.

"Phoebe, don't kick that sofa leg, it's an antique," Pascal scolded with some annoyance. Phoebe blushed and placed her tiny feet together and her hands in her lap. Imagining herself in one of Nora's corsets and gowns, she straightened her back and shoulders.

"That's better," he immediately noticed, and rewarded her good posture with a kiss.

For a couple of days Phoebe was so busy with fittings and rehearsals that she forgot about the locked room, but she did not forget the photo album, or the additional cache of esoteric erotica she found in William Random's library. She had already memorized the faces of all the people in the six spanking stills, in case she should run into any of them in town.

Meanwhile, Pascal had begun his photographic odyssey with an inn and pub-crawl from Random Point to Provincetown.

His first stop was The Dummy Up Club, which was all but hidden in the woods about two miles out of town. Rustic but luxurious, the house included a piano bar, a billiards room and restaurant. He wanted to photograph the humidor. The moment he entered he heard a voice he recognized, backed up by an accomplished pianist, rendering a Harold Arlen song that always gave him chills. As Pascal followed the enchanting sounds to their source he discovered his wife, gloriously clad in a pale blue portrait collar dress, sitting on the piano bench beside the musical composer Anthony Newton.

Pascal wandered over to the bar and ordered a scotch. Phoebe hadn't noticed him yet but this did not surprise him, considering her important quarry. He knew that Anthony Newton owned a house in Random Point, but never guessed he'd be accessible. No doubt he'd been playing when Phoebe arrived. (She'd never told him she was going to the Dummy Up Club after rehearsal!) And Phoebe had seized the opportunity to demonstrate the range of her classically trained voice to the handsome maestro.

Pascal sat at the bar, unnoticed by the performers, who had a small audience scattered throughout the lounge and adjoining dining room. "I wonder who she is," said a young and naughty looking blonde in a white halter dress who slid onto the barstool beside Pascal.

"She's my wife," he told her, introducing himself.

"That name is familiar. Are you the couple who are renting William Random's house?" When Pascal confirmed that they were, she said, "I'm William's former sister-in-law, Susan Ross," and shook his hands with him vigorously.

"And that's my boyfriend, Anthony Newton. Your wife is ravishing. Are you worrying right now?"

"I might be if I didn't have you as a hostage," he struck a match to light her cigarette. Susan tossed back two and half feet of silky, goldenrod hair with a smile.

"Wouldn't they make a glorious plate for your book?" she asked, for she knew all about William's autumn tenants and why they were in Random Point.

"Sensational, but I make it a policy never to torment celebrities."

"I'll go and ask permission!" Susan jumped off her stool without waiting for a reply. They had just finished the song and were about to start another when Susan appeared at Anthony's elbow.

"Hello," said Susan with a warm smile for Phoebe.

Anthony introduced the two young women.

"You know, you two look so picture perfect together that it would be a shame not to let Mr. Robbins photograph you for his book,"

Susan suggested.

"Mr. Robbins?" Anthony asked.

"That handsome man at the bar, who also happens to be this lady's husband," Susan said, smiling brightly at Phoebe, who stared at Susan for a few seconds as though she recognized her, then suddenly did recognize her, then blushed deeply.

"I don't mind," said Anthony, waving at Pascal to come over. Another introduction was made. Pleased at his sudden fortune, Pascal rushed out to his car to get a couple of lights.

Phoebe wanted to communicate with her husband at once, but didn't dare abandon her precious seat on the bench beside the composer. An intimate portrait of herself and Anthony Newton would provide golden publicity for a girl whose objective was Broadway. Besides, Mr. Newton had magic. She felt it the moment she sat down beside him. And now that she had recognized Susan, a tinge of eroticism was added. Phoebe longed to know the details of Anthony Newton's relationship with the adorable 22-year-old blonde who had appeared so submissively in William Random's photo album.

Driving the short distance home down heavily wooded Shadow Lane, the tightness in Pascal's jaw line alerted Phoebe that a lecture was coming.

"Is something the matter, darling?" she queried, receiving a glare for her pains.

"You bet something is the matter," he replied firmly, pulling into the driveway beside the Random house. Phoebe thought what a splendid Torvald her own husband would have made, had he only taken up the stage.

She locked the door behind them and followed him into the sitting room, where he immediately poured himself a scotch. She shuddered at the possible increase in husbandly belligerence this additional shot might spur, though she did admire his capacity. Alcohol did not agree with Phoebe, as she harshly rediscovered at least once a year.

"I just remembered, there's something I must show you!" Phoebe ran out of the room and returned a minute later with the photo album.

"Phoebe, I'm not in the mood," he snapped, lighting a cigarette. "What was the idea of swarming all over Anthony Newton tonight?"

"I beg your pardon?"

"I believe the term is, kissing up, unless you were all over that annoyingly wealthy and attractive man for some reason other than career advancement, in which case, I may well lose my temper."

"And what happens then?"

"You don't want to know," he promised, pouring another.

"We got a photo for the book, didn't we?" she cajoled, putting the album down.

"Yes," he admitted without pleasure. "But I still want to know why."

"Why what, darling?"

"Why you were practically sitting on Anthony Newton's lap all night."

"I was doing no such thing."

"You sang for ninety minutes. Fifteen would have been plenty. Then we lingered for two hours over a dinner we should have declined. On top of which, you simpered and cooed until I thought I would be sick."

"I thought I made a nice impression," said returned mildly, delighted by his jealousy.

"Not on me, you didn't."

"We got invited for tennis."

"Swell."

"Darling, don't you agree that this is about the best connection I'm ever likely to make?" Phoebe asked, sitting in front of the album again and casually opening it to the page with Susan's picture. Yes, it was the same girl, except in the photo she had a ponytail.

"Yes, I agree," he grudgingly admitted, "but that's no reason for you to throw yourself at him."

"I did no such thing!" she jumped to her feet and cried. "And you had better apologize for that remark."

"Me apologize?" he laughed contemptuously and again Phoebe thought what a shame it was the stage had missed Pascal, because he was as great a ham as she'd ever met.

"That's right," she haughtily replied, "and until you do, I will remain incommunicado!" With this she picked up the heavy album, tucked it under her arm and made her exit.

Pascal slammed his glass down and followed her. "Phoebe, don't you dare walk out on me while we're having an argument!" he stopped her half way up the staircase. "And why are you still dragging that around?" he gestured at the ubiquitous album, becoming somewhat annoyed at its fascination for his wife.

"What the Necronomicon was to Arkham, this book is to Random Point, and I must avail myself of its secret knowledge while I possess it," she announced bafflingly and quickly ran up the stairs to lock herself into a bedroom other than the one they'd been sharing. If she'd just begun speaking in tongues, Pascal could not have been more dumbfounded. "Phoebe, open this door," he demanded, rapping smartly.

"No!" she said, curling up on a recamier and opening the album to Susan's page again. Outside the door, Pascal took a deep breath and forced himself to think logically.

"Nora wouldn't lock the door on Torvald," he gravely observed. "At least not in Act I." Before he had lit a new cigarette the door opened. Pascal strode in, fairly crackling with masculine energy. "That's better," he commented.

"Remember," she warned him, "Nora turns everything around at the end of Act III."

"Phoebe, what the hell did that comment on the stairs mean?"

"Are you really ready to listen?"

"Sure," he flung himself into a wing chair.

"Do you recognize her?" she asked, showing him the photograph of Susan.

"She looks awfully familiar," he admitted.

"That's Susan Ross, the young lady we spent two hours with tonight."

"I suppose it is," he agreed, looking closely at the photograph. "But what of it? You heard her say that she was William Random's sister-in-law. Why shouldn't her photo show up in his album?"

"In this kind of album?"

"Why not?'

"I just find it extremely interesting," Phoebe insisted, turning over another page or two. Pascal found himself staring at the photos along with her, until one caught his eye.

"She looks familiar too," said Pascal, pointing to a still of a corseted blonde bound to a whipping post while a tall, Celtic god used a flogger on her bare backside.

"Does she? Where did you see her? Did you meet her in the village? Think!" Phoebe was wild with excitement.

"I know," he snapped his fingers. "Come with me," he said, taking her by the hand and pulling her after him down the hall, up a narrow wooden staircase and into a custom darkroom. Inside he switched on the light to reveal a gallery of black and white stills clothes-pinned to a line. "Here she is!" he seized one of the stills.

"It's the girl who's renting the light house I photographed yesterday. Her name is Patricia Fairservis." Pascal showed Phoebe the shot of a pouty blonde, sitting in the window seat of her lighthouse studio. "Beginning to see a pattern?" she demanded.

"No."

"I believe that sooner or later we're going to meet everyone who shows up in this album, and in doing so uncover the best-heeled little B&D community in the commonwealth."

"The best-heeled little what?"

"Pascal, please don't tell me that you've never heard of B&D?" she sighed condescendingly.

"Sure I've heard of it," he said, flipping through the album as he desperately tried to recall what the letters stood for.

"Oh? So, tell me what you think it is."

"It's," he hesitated for a moment, gazing at a photo in the album, his memory was jogged by the image of little Damaris being buckled into a bondage collar while stretched across the lap of William Random and he triumphantly blurted out, "bondage and discipline!"

"Oh, so you do know," she replied, with some surprise.

"I suppose you see these nice perverts of Random Point as some sort of sadomasochistic coven grooming you for their sacrificial alter?" he ventured.

"No, of course not," she protested.

"Oh yes you do. I see what's happening here. It's the Rosemary's

Baby Syndrome all over again. Fanciful actress senses dangerous conspiracy, sees herself as next ritual victim. Next thing you know, you'll be kidnapped, raped and impregnated by the head satyr, (Anthony Newton, no doubt), while I sell my soul to this one here," he indicated a sartorially elegant gentleman spanking Susan Ross in one of the photos.

"Let's see if any of your other photos match the ones in the album," Phoebe said, ignoring his hypothesis to scan the stills. "And yes, I've found another!" she pulled down a shot of several patrons sitting in the pub at The Bone and Feather Inn, one of whom appeared to be the same tow-headed monument of a man who'd wielded the whip in the photo of Patricia Fairservis. "Isn't this the fellow with the flogger?" she demanded.

"Looks similar," Pascal conceded.

"And here's another one!" she cried, pulling down a photo Pascal had taken of a stunning young woman on the gallery steps of the finest bookshop in the village. "Who is she, Pascal?"

"That's Marguerite Alexander, the owner of the bookshop I photographed two days ago," he told her, comparing the still he took with a shot in the album of this statuesque beauty in a spider web gown, using a martinet on a charming brunette, who was cuffed to an X-frame.

"You see what I'm telling you?" Phoebe demanded.

"I see that certain people in the village happened to attend a wild party at which some photographs were taken," he conceded, "but how do you know it wasn't some sort of Halloween hijinks?"

"Then what about the other photos in the album, the studio shots? How do you account for those?'

"William Random's hobby is erotic photography. What's so unusual about that?"

"Nothing, except for the quantity and quality of his models. Pascal. I really believe these are lifestylers," she insisted, riveted by the photos Pascal had taken.

"Well, just don't go asking," he warned.

"But, why not?"

"Because besides being prurient, it's none of our business."

"I suppose you're right," she murmured.

"I still don't understand why you're so fixated on that album anyway," he said, leading her out of the dark room and closing the door behind them. "People have a right to be as kinky as they choose."

"Oh, I wholly agree!" she replied, linking arms with her husband as they returned together to the bedroom they'd been sharing.

"So why are you obsessing on them?"

"Because maybe I'm a little kinky myself," she answered slowly.

"Oh, are you?" he laughed affectionately for the first time that evening.

"Just a little," she blushed deeply as her heart began to race.

"Just a little, eh?" He folded his arms and looked her up and down. "Well then maybe I should turn you over my knee and give you just a little spanking for flirting with Anthony Newton all night!"

"But, I didn't flirt," she lamely replied, her wide eyes following his every movement as she unconsciously pressed her back against a dresser.

"Oh yes you did! Come over here, young lady," he commanded, seizing her by her slender wrist and pulling her over to the upholstered bench at the foot of the bed, whereupon he sat down and very easily pulled her across his lap.

Phoebe didn't utter the slightest protest as he fastened one hand to her waist and brought the other one down on her skirted backside a half dozen times rather firmly. He expected her to struggle and beg him to stop, but she merely gasped and whimpered, without making a move to escape.

If he was momentarily puzzled, the melting look she cast him over one bare shoulder cleared the mystery and he realized with a start that she really wanted this.

Carefully pushing her skirt up to her waist, he discovered that his wife was clad in a blue satin corset with garter straps and seamed hose. As Pascal was something of a fetishist himself, the sight of these exquisite undergarments stimulated him immensely and he stroked her small, but extremely well rounded bottom gently with the palm of his hand. A blue satin g-string afforded her a tiny measure of modesty, but her bottom was now effectively bare.

"I didn't know you owned a corset," he commented with approval.

"I don't. This one belongs to the girl who lives here," Phoebe admitted. "We're almost the same size."

"Phoebe!" Smack! Smack! Smack! "You can't borrow an intimate garment like a corset without permission." Now he delivered ten or a dozen more spanks to her satiny cheeks, which instantly pinkened deeply, for she was very fair.

"Ow!" she cried, at last. His hand felt very different on her bare skin. It really imparted a sting. But oh, how heavenly it felt to finally be in this position, held fast and properly spanked for the first time and by Pascal! Phoebe squirmed as her husband's hand came down hard again and again. "I'll have it cleaned," she promised.

"I'll be happy to buy you some corsets," he told her, stopping to rub her pink cheeks. "But if I ever find out you've ransacked our landlady's closets again I'll take my razor strop to you." Pascal actually owned one. "Understand?"

"Yes, sir!" she immediately replied, causing him to smile. He seemed to have discovered an extremely important secret about his Phoebe.

"I'd expect that kind of behavior from a common sort of girl, but you're supposed to be a lady," he continued to scold her; reveling in the authority she had suddenly given him. Not to mention her reaction to the spanking. He thought he had seen her aroused before, but this sort of response made their wedding night look like a still life.

"You know, Phoebe, I've found you somewhat intractable in the past, but now I realize I've just been taking the wrong approach with you," he informed her, administering another volley of vigorous smacks to her bottom cheeks and upper thighs. "This is what I should have done whenever you were impossible. And this is what I will do from now on!"

When Pascal observed her not arguing, a splendid surge of power coursed through him, resolving itself into a large, pulsating erection. He spanked her until his arm began to tire, about fifteen minutes by the chiming mantle clock. When he finally released her, her bottom glowed magenta and was radiant from the tops of her thighs to the crest of her hips.

He had no idea of what had gone through her head during this procedure, but a good many sensations had passed through his own, from the thrill of mastery to the satisfaction of instilling some discipline into his exasperating beloved.

After letting her up he turned her around to undo her dress, which buttoned down the back. "Stand still," he told her as she fidgeted on her high heels. The dress fell to the floor and he turned her around to admire her dainty torso, so beautifully defined by the corset, which had a built-in brassiere to support her perfect bosom. "Let me look at you," he ordered as she blushed. "I've never seen you quite like this before, Phoebe, all flushed and fluttery. How do you account for it?" he demanded, while deliberately reaching into her bra and gently pinching each cherry nipple while she squirmed.

"I couldn't say," she replied, closing her eyes with a shiver as his hands traveled down to squeeze her nipped waist.

"Well, I'll tell you how I account for it," he said, suddenly standing up and deliberately bending her over the bench. "You've been waiting all this time for me to take control." He placed her palms on the seat of the bench, made her arch her back and separate her legs. "Now that I've started to do it," he said, smacking her hard on either cheek, "you're just a little bit scared. Am I right?"

"Yes, that's what makes it sexy," she thought to herself but instead shook her head in denial. Pascal laughed. Then she heard his zipper come down and felt him against her. In a moment he'd pulled the scrap of g-string aside and plunged his engorged cock inside her to the hilt. Pulling her up by the hips, he drove in even deeper, locking her against him with a hand pressed to her corseted abdomen. The placement of his palm directly atop her g-spot, in combination with the firm thrusts of his organ brought her to the edge of climax almost immediately, then promptly sent her crashing over it.

"Never!" she breathed, when he finally let her go, a few minutes later, having ejaculated deep inside her creamy core.

"Never what?" he wanted to know, helping her to stand again.

"Never have I felt anything so moving, so utterly cataclysmic!" she declared, throwing herself into his arms.

"Never have I felt you come so fast," he observed, as she went behind a wood framed screen to slip into a silk nightgown.

"Do you know what I plan to do, darling?" Phoebe asked as she climbed into bed beside him a minute later.

"No, what?" he pulled her against him contentedly; ready to slip off to sleep. "I'm going to spend the summer tracking down every person in the Random photo album and making them my friends."

"Good girl," he murmured drowsily. An instant later he sat up and stared at her. "What did you say?"

"I said I was going to find everyone in the album and introduce myself to them."

"But to what end?"

Phoebe thought, "Mine, actually," but chose not to share this bad joke as she noticed Pascal's growing unease. Instead she replied nonchalantly, as though she'd already lost interest in the subject, "Oh, they just seem like my kind of people."

"Phoebe, I don't like this," he said, lighting a cigarette.

"Don't like what?"

"Don't like the idea of you tracking down every B&D player in the village. What do you intend to do with them once you unearth them, eh?"

"I'd just like to get to know them. After all, we'll be spending three months in Random Point. Doesn't it make sense to socialize with the most sophisticated couples in town?"

"Are you sure you don't mean socialate?" he brooded.

"What does that mean?"

"What do you suppose is going to happen when you open Pandora's Box?"

"I don't know."

"But you want and expect something to happen, don't you?"

"I wouldn't mind getting invited to one of those parties."

"One of which parties?"

"The kind at which the album pictures were taken."

"I see." Crushing out the cigarette, Pascal laced his hands behind his head and stared out the window at the rustling trees and half moon.

"Pascal?"

"Yes?"

She burrowed against his side until he drew her into his arms. "You'll never know how much that meant to me," she confided, shuddering with the memory of the spanking and sex.

"And don't think that'll be the last time either," he warned her, hugging her closer. "Not with brainstorms like yours."

"I must admit, if there's any place a girl like me could get into trouble, it's Random Point," she mused.

"You know, unfaithful wives were pilloried in Random Point until 1797." Pascal informed her, "I looked that up in the town charter. The pillory still stands today. I intend to photograph it later in the summer. Just be careful I don't get a notion to lock my favorite actress into it when I do."

Chapter Six

Phoebe and Pascal Part 2

Phoebe's Torvald was a tall, lanky, neatly bearded and rambunctiously jovial emoter, around her husband's age, who took to his new leading lady immediately. It was difficult to imagine such a big-hearted man portraying a stern, judgmental character like Torvald, but as soon as he stepped out on the stage he accomplished the metamorphosis ably.

One afternoon, as they were rehearsing their opening scene, where Torvald accuses Nora of eating chocolate macaroons, Phoebe happened to notice a stranger in the back of the small theatre, walking around the perimeter.

"Who's that?" Phoebe asked the production manager, for she suddenly seemed to recognize the warrior in natty tweeds across the rows of empty seats. It was the man in the photo album pictured flogging the blonde from the lighthouse.

"Oh, that's former detective Michael Flagg. He's installing a security system in the theatre this week," Todd replied.

As he heard his name mentioned, Michael waved at the little group on the stage. "Don't mind me," he said, "I'm just taking some measurements."

Phoebe and Michael exchanged lingering smiles across the theatre. Then she suddenly turned to her co-star and said, "You know, Rene, I've had some thoughts about this chocolate moment."

"Share them with me," the actor encouraged her.

"Well, in the Julie Harris teleplay of Doll's House from the 50's, Nora gets a little slap on the hand. Remember?"

"I do," Rene replied.

"Do you know what I think would be even more provocative?" Phoebe asked.

"What? I can't wait to hear."

"Why, if Torvald turned Nora over on his knee and gave her a few spanks?"

Though she didn't dare to look at him, Phoebe noticed out of the corner of her eye that Michael Flagg had stopped measuring doorways.

"I like that," Rene approved the suggestion at once. "Makes it sexier, doesn't it?" the actor appealed to their director, Clara Harte.

"I'm not sure the scene's ever been done that way before," that fair young woman mused, "but I see nothing to oppose the interpretation. Especially since we've decided to stress the eroticism in the relationship."

As Phoebe and Rene began to block out the business she hoped that Pascal would choose any other afternoon than this to drop in. In fact, it would suit her very well if he didn't discover her on-stage spanking until opening night.

As she hoped and expected, Michael Flagg was waiting for her outside the theatre when she departed at dusk.

"Oh, Mr. Flagg, you're just the person I wanted to see," Phoebe confessed in a rush.

"Great," he replied enthusiastically, for he hadn't come up with any legitimate excuse for waiting for her and knew very well that she was married.

"I'm Phoebe Casper," she extended her hand to be shaken. "I understand you're a former police detective? I do have a valid reason for asking."

"Well, yes," he smiled.

"And you do security now?'

"Occasionally."

"In that case, I think I'd like to hire you for a consultation."

"Oh really? What about?"

"Stalking," she declared dramatically. "I am an actress, you know. And I suddenly realized that I don't know the first thing about dealing with stalkers."

"You could probably benefit from some security advice. Shall we make an appointment?"

"What about tomorrow afternoon? You could come to the house," she suggested, knowing that Pascal would be in Boston.

"You're staying at William Random's, aren't you?" Michael asked, making a note in a small book.

"I see you know all about me already," she said with surprise.

"I ran into William before he left for Europe and he told me," Michael explained, adding, "If I'm not mistaken, your husband photographed me at the pub last week."

"Yes, I believe he did."

"Does he know you're engaging me to counsel you on stalkers?"

"Why, no," Phoebe replied, flushing violently as his question reminded her of how naughty she was being. Michael merely smiled and told her he would see her the following day.

Phoebe had coffee ready for Michael Flagg's arrival. She served it in the sitting room, where they held their consultation.

"Oh, I never did ask you what you're going to charge me for this," she said pleasantly, carefully watching his reaction to her first pot of real coffee.

"Mmmm," he said. "Good." Phoebe smiled.

"I wasn't going to charge you anything."

"Really? That's awfully nice of you."

"I can't wait to see you in the play," he confessed, unable to forget her pointed suggestion of adding a spanking to the business.

"I'll send you tickets for opening night."

"Thanks!"

"Michael, may I ask you something?" she asked suddenly, dragging the photo album over to him.

"Sure."

"Is this you?" Phoebe opened the album to the photo of Michael whipping Patricia.

"Yes, that's me," he replied immediately. "Let me see that, though." He took the album and flicked through some other pages.

"I guess you know everyone in there, huh?" she eagerly asked.

"I do," he replied, turning the pages with interest.

"Won't you tell me about them?" Phoebe brought Michael and the album back to the sofa, so they could turn the pages together.

"Sure. That's my ex-wife Damaris. She lives with William now, as you know. That's William's ex-wife Laura, she's Hugo Sands' girlfriend now. The four of them are vacationing in Europe together. Here's Hugo spanking Susan Ross, she's Laura's younger sister and Anthony Newton's girlfriend."

"I've met them!" she eagerly replied. "But there are no photos of Mr. Newton in this book. I suppose it would be too much to hope that he might be part of the group?"

"He's in it, all right, but he makes it a point not to get photographed doing anything scene-related because of his public image."

"Oh, I can imagine," Phoebe breathed reverently. "Do you think he would have minded me asking that question and you telling me the answer?"

"No," Michael replied with perfect confidence, "I'm sure he wouldn't. Now, this girl here is Marguerite Alexander," he returned to show and tell with the album, "She owns the bookshop. She's in and out of town because her husband's business is Boston-based. The young lady she's whipping is Diana Stratton; she's Susan's best friend. You'll probably meet her before too long. In fact, I'll make sure they all come to your opening night. The lady with me in this photo is my girlfriend, Patricia Fairservis. She lives in the lighthouse."

"She's glorious."

"Spoiled though."

"I'm surprised she has the nerve to be if you're her boyfriend."

"It isn't so much nerve as will."

"Well, thanks for filling me in. I've been looking at the photographs a good deal lately and wondering about all of you."

"What sort of things have you been wondering?"

"Mainly what it would take to become one of the clique," she answered frankly.

"What clique?"

"The B&D clique in the village."

"Why? Do you play?"

"I don't know. What does that mean?"

"This afternoon it meant getting Rene to spank you on stage, again and again. Quite an accomplishment for a novice. I was impressed."

"Did you enjoy watching us block out the scene?"

"You made him go through it ten times." Michael accurately recalled. "Three swats were given each time. And each time you encouraged Rene to smack you a little harder. Yes, I enjoyed watching that very much. Why do you think I waited for you afterwards?"

"I knew I recognized you from the book," she replied breathlessly.

"But tell me something, Phoebe, does Pascal share your interest in domestic discipline?"

"A little, I think. That is, although he never seemed the slightest bit inclined before we came to Random Point, now I think he may be a natural," she sagely reported.

"In that case, maybe we should return to the subject of security," Michael suddenly decided. "I installed an excellent system in this house myself.

Let me show you how it works."

Michael led Phoebe through the house, showing her alarms and hidden cameras. "Any room that has a TV or monitor is linked to the security camera system," Michael pointed out as they entered the master bedroom. He picked up the remote and tuned in to the security camera channel. Every few seconds, a different view of the outside of the house flashed across the screen. Then all four views would share the same screen for five more seconds before beginning again.

"See, Phoebe," Michael said, "this way you can tell if anyone has followed you home and is lurking around outside."

The camera facing the woods behind the house only showed a few squirrels.

The cameras focused on the sides of the house were watching flowers grow.

But the camera trained on the front door showed Pascal walking briskly up the walk to put his key in the lock.

"Oh dear," said Phoebe, her heart nearly stopping. "Let's go downstairs!" she preceded Michael out the door in a small flash.

Pascal registered immediate displeasure upon entering the house and encountering Michael Flagg descending the stairs with Phoebe.

"Hi, dear," Phoebe cried, rushing down to greet him. "You remember Michael Flagg, from the pub?"

"Sure. How are you?" Pascal put out his hand to shake Michael's and pretended he wasn't annoyed.

"Michael installed the security system in this house and he was showing me how everything works," Phoebe revealed brightly.

"Actually, we'd just finished, but I'd be happy to give you a quick run down as well," Michael offered.

"I'm sure Phoebe can explain it to me herself," Pascal said, staring pointedly at his trembling wife. "But will you stay for a drink?"

"No thanks, Phoebe gave me coffee. See you two soon, I hope," Michael pleasantly said, slipping out the door.

The instant it had closed Pascal turned an x-ray gaze on Phoebe and demanded, "What was he doing here?"

"Showing me the security system," she replied, less brightly than before.

"By your invitation?" he snapped.

"Well, yes," she timidly admitted, thoroughly cowed by the thundercloud that had formed upon her husband's brow.

"I see!" Pascal strode into the sitting room to make himself a drink, not failing to notice and scowl at the coffee service that she had somehow managed to properly utilize for once.

Half a drink had already disappeared down his throat when she hesitantly followed him into the room, a blush of guilt suffusing her face.

"Phoebe, what have you been up to?" he asked, in a tone now slightly less overwrought, as the well known comfortable glow spread through every fiber.

"Nothing at all. Not the slightest thing," she assured him.

"What's this doing here?" Pascal gestured at the album.

"It's always here. This is the room it lives in," she replied truthfully.

"You quizzed him on the album, didn't you?"

Looking both sullen and guilty, Phoebe made no reply.

"You invited Michael Flagg over, ostensibly to find out about the security system, and wound up discussing B&D in Random Point. Is that the correct scenario?"

"Pretty much so. Only we hardly said two words about anything when you came home."

"Where did you run into him that you had the opportunity to invite him home with you?"

"Must you put it quite that way?" she bristled, biting off a large chunk of chocolate covered macaroon for every swig of scotch he took.

"Where, Phoebe?"

"He happened to be at the theatre during today's rehearsal."

"And what were you two doing upstairs just now?"

"He was just showing me how the security cameras hook up to all the TV's in the house. That's all."

"I don't believe you."

"But, Pascal, it's the absolute truth."

"I don't trust you."

"I'm sorry." She hung her head.

"I was half way to Boston when I realized I'd arranged to shoot that leather bar in P-town this evening."

"Should I come and meet you there after rehearsal?"

"No. It's a gay bar. No one would want to pose for me if I dragged my frou-frou wife in there."

"Oh."

"I'm sure I'll be home before ten," he told her, finishing his drink then leaving her. Phoebe started after him in confusion, unable to define his mood. She followed him out to his car as he loaded in his lights.

"Darling? You're not angry at me, are you?" she caught his hand, brought it to her lips and kissed it. He melted instantly and pulled her into his arms to thoroughly kiss her.

"You'll find out when I get home tonight," he told her, letting her go abruptly.

"Maybe you'll cool off by then,' she suggested as he got into his convertible. "I want you to come home straight after rehearsal," he warned her sternly.

"I will, Pascal," she promised.

"I suppose you'd better stop in town for dinner first," he amended, "but come home right after that. Understand?"

"Yes, darling."

"And no male escorts."

"No, dear."

Pascal roared off in his sports car, leaving Phoebe trembling in the wake of his various orders and implied threats. He almost sounded as if he intended to punish her when he returned home that night!

After the rehearsal, Phoebe defied Pascal's orders and went out with some of the cast for dinner at The Bone and Feather. But she made sure to arrive home three minutes before ten.

It was nearly midnight before Pascal joined her there.

"Well," she declared, "the boys must have really liked you!"

"I got some great photos."

"I hope you didn't have to put out."

"Go ahead, add insult to injury," he warned her, opening the balcony doors and strolling out into the moonlight. She came out beside him and rubbed up against him in her slippery, cream satin pajamas.

"I've been waiting and waiting for you," she complained, squirming as he wound one hand in her hair and kissed her.

"I'm as inclined to beat you as kiss you," he scowled, pushing her away and lighting a cigarette.

"Well, darling, can't you do both?"

"Did you confide to Flagg what you're about?"

"I don't know what you mean, dear."

"You said you showed him the album, asked him questions. Didn't he wonder why?"

"I don't know."

"I can easily imagine why you'd invite that man over when you knew I was going to be away."

"My intentions were strictly honorable."

"That's what you always say, but I happen to know differently."

"Oh really?"

"When you want to get a man's attention you flirt!"

"If I wanted to get Mr. Flagg's attention it was only to discover more about the album in general rather than him in particular, and I assure you that I didn't flirt."

"And I suppose if he weren't the gym-hewn monolith that he is you'd have invited him home just as readily?" When Phoebe hesitated a moment in replying, he cried, "Right! You little baggage."

"I'm nothing of the sort," she replied with hauteur.

"Oh yes you are."

"Pascal, say you're not really upset with me."

"But I am upset," he replied stubbornly.

"I only asked him over to converse."

"Yeah, so you said."

Phoebe sighed and wandered back into the bedroom, unable to determine, as usual, what her husband's mood really was. She got into bed and pulled the covers up to her chin. In a minute he came in, dimmed the lights and began to undress.

"One more incident like this and you're going in that pillory," he promised before getting into bed.

A few days later Pascal was canvassing the village when he stumbled across Hugo Sands' Antiques shop and discovered the remarkably beautiful young lady who was to become his next model.

Pamela Crane, who had been polishing an old clock, was thrilled to admit the photographer into the shop, especially when he promised to credit Sands' Antiques when his book came out. No sooner had Pascal taken a good look at Pamela than he decided to offer her a season of modeling work, which she enthusiastically accepted.

"You can quit worrying about the town stocks," Pascal informed Phoebe with ill-concealed excitement that evening over dinner at a pleasant Woodbridge roadhouse. "I've found a girl who'll go into them willingly, in Puritan dress, and she's willing to run up the costume herself." Then Pascal launched into a detailed description of the extraordinary creature he'd found in Random Point that afternoon.

"She must be 5'10", with hair like black silk and legs from here to heaven. And what a face, what style, what fashion sense. I tell you,

I've made a discovery, and she's all mine," Pascal reported blithely to his smolderingly jealous 5'3" spitfire. "I've decided to devote a complete section of the book to historical tableaux, with my girl Pamela in period attire."

"I look good in period attire. Can't I be in that portion of the book too?"

Phoebe startled him by asking.

"Well, dear, you're already going to be in that handsome full page still with Anthony Newton," he explained. "But this Pamela person is marvelous enough to have a whole section of tableaux just devoted to her?"

"Phoebe, don't be childish, she's a model, as I've told you. She's got the face and figure to plug into any fantasy. I see her as clay."

"Does that mean you'll be kneading and stretching her a lot?"

"Phoebe, don't start."

"Don't start what? And yes, I will have some wine," she declared, defiantly holding out her glass to be filled.

"Don't start throwing a jealous tantrum about one of my models."

"Oh, I'm not jealous of some vapid mannequin."

"This one isn't vapid. She's been to the best schools and has impeccable taste."

Phoebe regarded her own reflection in a mirror opposite. Her white and yellow sundress had a laced bodice and full cotton skirt. "You're getting better," Pascal told her, noticing her self-appraisal.

"Oh go to hell!" she snapped, infuriated by everything he had told her.

The next day Phoebe could not prevent herself from stopping by Hugo Sands' Antiques in order to meet and interview the young lady who had captivated Pascal the previous day. She found that his description of Pamela's grace and elegance had not been exaggerated; she was the personification of glamour.

Phoebe was not ready to be disarmed by Pamela, but this was exactly what happened.

"I understand you're to be Nora and you're looking for a proper corset. Did you know there's a wonderful little corsetiere in P-town? I have a card."

Pamela handed Phoebe a card for a Provincetown corset shop. "Bring a hundred and fifty dollars and you'll go home in heaven. You can teach your handsome husband how to lace you and be down to 22" by opening night."

"Gosh, that's a lot of money," said Phoebe doubtfully, at which Pamela stared.

"But it will last for years," the willowy one explained with reverence. "And I can't wait to see you cinched."

Phoebe glowed with vanity. She had never been stroked by another woman before and the approach suddenly turned her rival into a girlfriend.

"Pascal says you know a lot about outfits."

"Pascal says his wife's a tomboy," Pamela smiled, "but he wishes she weren't."

"Well, I'm an impoverished actress," Phoebe defended herself. "I wasn't even able to quit waitressing until I married Pascal, no less think about spending hundreds of dollars on lingerie at a time."

"An excellent corset is a basic piece of wardrobe equipment," Pamela informed her new friend firmly. "You'll learn. I'll help you. You're so gorgeous with just nothing, by the time I get through with you, you'll be a goddess."

"Really? In what way?"

"What I could do with braids, pearls and your hair," Pamela mused.

"Thanks, but you're the one who's amazing," Phoebe acknowledged, thoroughly tamed by her new friend. "And I understand you're also the one who's going to save me from the pillory."

Pamela smiled. "I've never walked by that pillory without thinking of being locked into it!"

"You mean with a sense of social outrage?" the actress queried casually.

"No, with a sense of arousal."

"You mean you're into discipline too?" Phoebe couldn't help but blurting out.

"Too?"

"Well, it seems there are a lot of people in Random Point who are into discipline."

"Oh, there are. Are you by any chance one of us, Phoebe?"

"I most ardently am!" Phoebe declared, finding this conversation even more satisfying than the one she'd had with Michael Flagg on the same subject.

"And your husband?" Pamela asked with great interest.

"Maybe," said Phoebe circumspectly. "I'm not really sure yet. Though he has spanked me once."

"I'm sure that was thrilling. Spanking is my favorite thing," the art school girl confessed.

"And how about you? Do you have a handsome husband who spanks you?"

"A fiancé," Pamela shyly replied, extending her slim, perfectly manicured hand to display a smart engagement ring. "And he is terribly handsome and wonderfully strict," she added, pulling Sloan's photo out of a small drawer.

"My, he is striking," Phoebe commented, of Pamela's logical counterpart.

"He works right across the street at the bookshop. You should go and introduce yourself. He worships Ibsen and we've already got our tickets for your opening night. Besides, I want him to see what a charming wife Pascal has. He's been a bit nervous since yesterday."

"But, you say this young man is your dominant?" Phoebe was intrigued and titillated as she stared at Sloan's photo. "How exciting it must be to be absolutely certain that your lover gets a thrill out of spanking you," Phoebe mused.

"I should think that anyone would get a thrill out of spanking you. Anyway, Pascal is certainly bossy enough," Pamela reflected.

"He intends to mold you. Like clay," Phoebe warned her new friend as she left to go across the street and visit the bookshop.

"Don't forget about the corset. Go tomorrow," Pamela called after her, then immediately dialed the bookshop.

"Alexander's Bookshop. Sloan speaking. May I be of some assistance?"

Pamela's intended cheerfully replied.

"Sloan. Pamela. Pascal Robbins' wife is about to enter your shop. And guess what, Sloan, she's into it!"

"Into it?"

"You know what I mean. She just walked in. See her?"

"Thank you so much," Sloan said, hanging up in time to greet Phoebe.

Two afternoons later Pascal sat in the window seat of their bedroom and smoked as Pamela demonstrated how to lace a waist cinch. Phoebe, dressed only in a cream lace bra and panty combination, balanced on her highest ankle strap heels as Pamela deftly hooked the five steel clasps in the front of the boned garment to fasten it, attached each of the eight garter straps to her sheer stockings, then turned her around to lace her up the back. The waist cinch was of sand colored cotton reptide and handsome.

"Now, watch carefully," Pamela told Pascal, "because you're going to have to do this for her the first four or five times, until she gets the knack of lacing herself."

"I'm all attention," said he, really riveted by the procedure of tightening the laces.

"Now then, your wife has a natural 24" waist. This corset will take her down four inches if she wears it a good deal and doesn't gain any weight. As it is, I can see her cinching comfortably to 22" in a few weeks. But let's start with a just an inch for now."

"It looks wonderful," he observed as Pamela pulled the laces, creating a classic, petite hourglass figure for Phoebe.

"Wear it just like that for an hour to two hours a day to start with," Pamela instructed. "After about a week you can tighten it up a bit and increase to three or four hours a day. I think you'll find the results remarkable."

But the next morning, when he was called upon to help Phoebe corset, Pascal was not in so mild a mood. For the previous night, at The Dummy Up Club, while Pascal had been photographing Pamela in a sophisticated evening gown, snipping a cigar between her satin-gloved hands, Phoebe had been keeping Sloan company in the bar.

And Pascal hadn't liked the way she did it. Sloan had only come along to keep his eye on Pamela, but now that the actress had learned what kind of man Sloan was, Phoebe was irresistibly drawn to him.

Besides, he was such a natural tease that it was impossible not to fall under his spell. Pascal couldn't help but notice.

He was too tired from shooting all day to take it up with Phoebe when they got home, but the following morning, while he was lacing her into her corset, it all came back to him and with determination he began to pull the strings a good deal more tightly than Pamela had recommended.

"Hey!" Phoebe cried, "That's too tight!"

"Nonsense. That's the way it's supposed to be," he said, tightening the laces down from her nipped waist to her flared hips. "The two sides should meet in the back completely."

"Not right away!" she gasped. "Please, darling, loosen me up!"

"Not right away," he told her firmly, and instead pulled her down across his lap. She hadn't yet donned bra, panties or stockings and her round, creamy bottom looked more naked for the framing of the glove tight cinch.

"What are you doing?" She squirmed to get away for she felt severely restricted and her bottom seemed to swell in protest of the constriction at the hips.

"Giving you a good spanking for behaving so badly at the bar last night," he declared, wrapping one hand around her greatly reduced waist and bringing the other down on her satiny backside eight or ten times hard. His hand left a dark pink imprint on each cheek and caused her to squirm across his lap. "There!" he said, putting her back on her feet. "I hope you felt those."

"I did!" she replied, with a trembling under lip that softened him instantly. "What's the matter?"

"Too tight and too hard," she sobbed, putting one hand back to rub her sore bottom.

"Oh, all right," he sighed, turning her around to loosen the laces with every evidence of annoyance, though his own heart pounded with excitement.

There was something about lacing her more tightly than she liked that had given him a perverse thrill.

He loosened the laces a little. "How's that?" he asked, as though he didn't much care how she responded.

"Still very tight," she breathed, suddenly realizing that he had chosen this method to (dare she apply the sacred word?) discipline her! Something about lacing her aroused him. Just knowing this thrilled her. "But, I suppose it will teach me better self control," she ventured timidly.

"My thought entirely," he agreed, this time only patting her bare backside and even kissing her there. "Look, how pink your bottom is, Phoebe," he told her. She looked over her shoulder into the wardrobe mirror to see.

After Pascal had gone, Phoebe got a tape measure and measured her waist.

He'd gotten her down to 22" on her second day. No wonder she was gasping for breath! The corset changed her carriage and her gait. She couldn't take her eyes off her image in the many mirrors of the house after she'd donned her bra and panties and a beige cotton sundress, which now draped so loosely that she had to add a belt.

When she went into the village she noticed men looking at her differently than they had the previous day. But her back was beginning to hurt and she felt she hadn't taken a really good breath since Pascal had laced her.

Therefore her first stop was the Antiques Shop, where she intended to have Pamela loosen her stays. But as she passed by the window she saw that she was foiled, because Pascal was inside, shooting one of the tableaux he'd spoken of, utilizing furnishings from the shop and a flawless Victorian costume Pamela had produced from her large and unusual wardrobe.

Now Phoebe was perplexed. It was too early to find anyone at the theatre and she simply couldn't stay another hour in the corset. Then she noticed Sloan in the window of bookshop across the street and realized she was saved. She rushed over to the store, quite unaware that at the moment she slipped through the door, Pascal chanced to look up and spot her.

When Phoebe rushed in Sloan was alone shelving paperbacks.

"Hi Sloan," said Phoebe in a rush, "would you do me a giant favor?"

"Of course," he smiled as he noticed how charming she looked that day.

"Do you know how to loosen stays?"

"Loosen stays? You mean a corset?"

"Yes. I have one on and it's laced so tightly that I feel as though I'm going to faint."

"I'd be happy to help, but are you sure you don't want to go across the street and have Pamela do it?"

"That's the problem, Sloan. Pascal is there with her now and he's the one who laced me this morning. I don't want him to know I can't wear it this tight."

"Okay, come in the back for a second," he told her, leading the way into his office.

Back in Hugo Sands' Antiques shop, Pascal had abandoned his lights and 4 x 5 camera to stare out the street side windows as he waited impatiently for Phoebe to emerge from the bookstore. "I wonder what she's doing in there so long," he mused aloud, going to the phone on the counter and asking Pamela for the number. She told him, he dialed and the phone rang without being answered.

Sloan had just unbuttoned the back of Phoebe's dress and was sitting on a chair with the actress before him preparing to loosen her laces, when the phone rang. "Since we have to work fast, I won't answer that," he told her, untying the bow at the hem of the corset and carefully pulling the laces open without completely undoing the snugly interlacing network of restriction. "My, this is tight," he observed. "What was Pascal thinking?"

Meanwhile the phone continued to ring.

Finally Pascal slammed the phone down and told Pamela, "I'll be right back." Then he marched out the door and across the street. As soon as he entered the bookstore, his heart began to pound violently. With an unerring sense of direction, Pascal ignored the aisles and rising galleries and walked straight into the back of the shop where the first office he came to yielded the pair he sought.

When Pascal entered Sloan's office the good-looking store

manager was just rebuttoning the last button at the top of Phoebe's dress.

"Pascal!" Phoebe cried, flushing scarlet.

"Phoebe, what's going on here?"

"Nothing, darling," she explained, stepping away from Sloan but no closer to Pascal, who looked furious.

"Phoebe's waist cinch was too tight and she asked me to loosen it," Sloan reported immediately.

"It's true, Pascal. That's the only reason I came in," she added meekly. "I see," her husband replied. "Even though Pamela and I were right across the street and could have done it just as easily for you?"

"Well, this morning you seemed so intent on lacing me tightly that I didn't want to disappoint you by admitting defeat so soon."

"So instead you invite another man to perform this intimate service for you while I'm not 20 yards away!" the photographer reproached his wife with mounting anger. Unusually sensitive and overwrought, due to the stringent corseting, Phoebe's eyes over spilled with tears.

"I have to get back to the floor," Sloan explained, leaving them alone.

"Phoebe, is this the way you behave when I'm on the road?" Pascal demanded.

"No," she tremblingly replied, taking a step backward lest he be tempted to slap her.

"I don't believe you," he snapped. "And what's more, I think you're a horrible flirt."

"That's not true!" Phoebe cried, wiping her eyes with the back of her hand.

He seemed to notice for the first time how upset she was.

"Phoebe, now look what you've done," he pulled her over to a mirror to show her how she'd smudged her mascara. The eye makeup was a new enhancement suggested by Pamela, and Phoebe was as unused to it as she was to her corset. Pascal dipped the edge of his clean white handkerchief in cold water and carefully removed the few specks of mascara she had displaced with her rubbing. "We can't have you going to rehearsal looking like a wreck," he told her firmly, unable then to keep his hands off her waist.

"What am I going to do with you?" he murmured, suddenly intensely aroused by her dear femininity.

Phoebe took as deep a breath as she could as she put her arms around Pascal and hugged him hard. Then they kissed and kissed. Finally he let her go.

"Come on," he told her, pulling her out of the shop by the hand, "I'm taking you to the theatre myself so you don't get up to any more mischief."

He put her in his car, drove her down the road and escorted her inside.

"Now remember, if you have to loosen those stays any more today, have one of the girls do it. Understand?" he held her hands as he gave her this command.

"Yes, darling."

"As soon as you get home tonight, we're going to have a long talk about how you let another man undress you," he warned firmly.

"We are?" she looked up at him in surprise, having nearly forgotten about Sloan.

"Phoebe, the fact that you went to Sloan today instead of Pamela and me is going to trouble me all day."

"But you seemed so unsympathetic when I asked you to loosen me up earlier," she protested. "And it really hurt!" she added, with a pout.

"Well, why didn't you say so?"

"But, I did and you ignored me."

"Nonsense. You never said it hurt."

"In the books I've been reading, when something hurts too much, the girl says 'mercy' and that way her -" Phoebe groped for the right word, "- dominant knows it's for real. Should I use that word next time?"

"Mercy!" he snorted. "That's what I've been showing too much of lately with you!" The next moment he was gone.

Phoebe had almost forgotten about the incident with Sloan when Pascal reminded her of it before bed. She had just come from her bath and was wearing a white cotton wrapper. Her hair nearly reached her waist in tight, glossy waves. He was sitting in the window seat smoking when she came to lean against him and stare out at the whispering trees. He put his arm around her waist and pulled her closer, but the feel of her tiny waist under his hand brought back the morning's events and instead of embracing her, he crushed out his cigarette and seized her by her slender shoulders.

"I just remembered something," he told her, pulling her straight across his lap. "You were a very bad girl this morning!" he told her, bringing his palm down first on one cheek and then the other, sharply through her thin robe. "Letting Sloan unlace you! You deserve a good spanking for that," he declared, bringing his hand down again a resounding dozen times.

"Do you really think so?"

"I most certainly do!"

"I may have been indiscreet, but my intentions were honorable."

"That's what you always say."

"I only wanted him to loosen my stays."

"And you don't think that's provocative?" Smack! Smack! "You think a nice, young, married lady behaves like that?" Smack! Smack! The spanking continued. "You should have come and asked Pamela or me to loosen your stays. You realize that now, don't you, Phoebe?"

"Yes, completely!" His hand was really starting to sting her tender flesh and she wriggled on his lap to avoid it.

"Good!" he let her up. "Now get to bed," he ordered. "And don't ever let me catch you alone with Sloan Taylor again."

Phoebe climbed into bed with a pout as Pascal undressed. "Whereas you get to be alone with Pamela as much as you like," Phoebe muttered, pulling the covers up to her waist.

"That's different, darling," he told her, getting into bed and pulling her into his arms. "That's work."

"Ha!" Phoebe turned on her side and so did he, pulling her back against him and pressing his cock into the valley between her bottom cheeks. "No!" she cried, pulling away.

"Relax, I'm not going to," he told her, guiding his cock down between her thighs to nudge the proper portal. "But why I can't sodomize my wife now and then, I'd like to know."

"But it would hurt too much," she protested, very wet from the spanking and all too ready to take his cock.

"Don't you trust me?"

"After the way you laced me today?"

"Phoebe, you cut me to the quick," Pascal sounded hurt, but his cock was athrob, so she knew he was only teasing her. "I want you that way," he insisted, while plunging into her pussy to the depths. "And some day I'm just going to ignore your protests and take you that way," he promised in a tone that pierced her with a dart of painful pleasure.

Ten days passed, changing the weather from Indian Summer to pungent Autumn. Phoebe began to lace herself and managed to reduce her waist to a comfortable 22" by opening night. Meanwhile, she received no additional spankings from Pascal and began to wonder, with an aching sense of frustration, if he'd forgotten completely about her intense interest in the subject.

Having become better friends with Pamela, she confided her anxieties to the willowy model as they walked in the woods together one chilly afternoon. "A week or so ago, he seemed to understand what I needed," Phoebe mused, "but since then he's made no move in that direction. How can I get him to play with me without asking him directly?"

Pamela laughed, "Just do something to irritate him!"

"You mean be deliberately bad?"

"Why not?"

"I don't dare. He has a vile temper."

"I know, I've been working with him," Pamela smiled.

"Listen, couldn't you talk to him for me? Explain about the spanking thing?"

"I could, but wouldn't it be more fun to get him to do it naturally?"

"But I don't want Pascal to think badly of me."

"Oh, he won't."

"Well, what should I do?"

"What made him spank you the last time?"

"Didn't I tell you? It was when he found out I'd asked Sloan to loosen my stays."

"Oh, that's right." The girls emerged from the woods onto the thin, rocky strip of white beach. "Jealousy will no doubt always be the keynote in your scenarios," Pamela sagely predicted. "But as we've already gone on the Sloan ride, let's pick someone different to torment Pascal with this time. How about your attractive leading man, Rene?"

"Rene's a married man."

"Excellent, makes you seem even naughtier. Now, let's think of some subtle way we can place the thought of Rene in Pascal's head."

"No, Pamela, let's think of something else. This idea is too dangerous. What if Pascal really thinks Rene is making a play for me and tells him off, or worse?"

"Just leave it to me," said Pamela.

On the following Saturday, Pamela and Pascal shot at The Murderer's Clock Inn, an old hotel with a fine pub. In between set-ups they drank Irish coffees at one of the tables and Pamela leafed through the local entertainment papers until she came to a full-page ad for the upcoming run of A Doll's House. The ad featured Phoebe most prominently, with Rene in the background, but this was enough for Pamela to work with. "That Rene Whitfield is certainly a fine figure of a man," she commented. "He must be all of 6'4"!"

"You really like beards?" Pascal looked at the photograph critically, having never thought of his wife's leading man as being particularly striking.

"Not just any beard, of course," Pamela remarked, "but this man has the head of a Greek coin. We really ought to get him for one of our tableaux, Pascal."

"Yes, I suppose you're right," the photographer replied, looking at the ad again.

"I'll bet Phoebe has a powerful crush on him," Pamela remarked. Pascal looked at her sharply.

"What?"

"She's so romantic and he's so heroic."

"Oh, nonsense," Pascal snapped, but the few words were enough.

Phoebe's opening night went beautifully. The play was enthusiastically received and afterwards Anthony Newton threw a party for the cast at his house on the cliff. Rene's wife, a large, sweet, New England craftswoman, had no love of crowds and spent the greater part of the evening wandering around the mansion and admiring the art which decorated the halls and rooms. Her absence from her husband's side at his moment of triumph displeased Pascal more than it did Rene, who was used to the retiring ways of his beloved.

That was not the only annoyance suffered by Pascal, who was still in knots over Nora's opening scene, which had included the little spanking over the chocolate macaroons. He didn't remember any spanking in A Doll's House; therefore it must have been at Phoebe's suggestion that the business got added in. This notion seemed to make Pascal's blood pressure rise.

It wasn't only the idea of another man laying hands on her that upset him, it was the thought of how many times she might have insisted the scene be rehearsed. He knew Phoebe's passionate nature and had already observed the effects of a spanking upon it. He knew he could rely on her faithfulness, but only up to a point. For example, he guessed that his wife would permit any man she allowed to spank her, to also embrace and possibly even kiss her. And perhaps it had already gotten that far with the beard.

Meanwhile, it was maddening not to be able to go up to Phoebe and shake the truth out of her, but there was no chance of that with this crowd surrounding them.

Finally Pascal was able to catch Phoebe as she ran downstairs, holding the skirt of her new party dress above her ankles with both hands.

"Phoebe!" he grabbed her bare elbow. "I want to talk to you!" He pulled her back up to the second floor landing and over to an upholstered bench in the hall.

"Oh, Pascal, I'm having the most wonderful night of my life!" she breathed joyfully, throwing her arms around his slim torso and pressing her cheek against his face.

"Never mind that," he snapped, holding her at arm's length, "What about that first act?"

"First act?" Phoebe was baffled.

"The spanking business in the first act. You didn't tell me about that."

"But, darling, there was nothing to tell," Phoebe protested, blushing instantly.

"There's never been a spanking in A Doll's House before. Why is there one now?"

Phoebe tried to think of an answer that would satisfy him.

"Well? You initiated that business, didn't you, Phoebe?"

"Well, what if I did? It worked," she replied confidently.

"I can't believe you thought up a thing like that just to get a thrill."

"Pascal, I didn't!" she protested, shocked to hear it put that way.

"And with a man who isn't your husband. In front of an audience, no less!"

Pascal got up and paced.

"Really, darling, it was in the context of the play, after all."

"And what an audience. You must have realized you were turning half of them on," he accused, remembering all the players from the album that had been in attendance that night.

"The theatre is supposed to excite the senses," Phoebe declared firmly; "My director permitted my input because she agreed that it worked. She didn't accuse me of pandering!"

"That's just because she doesn't know your true leanings."

At that moment a tremendous voice booming Old Man River began to issue from the music room, accompanied by Anthony Newton on piano.

"I'll bet that's Rene," Phoebe fondly remarked, "he's got the most marvelous voice."

"You used to say I had the most marvelous voice," Pascal brooded.

"Oh, darling, but you do! It's practically the most thrilling thing about you!" Phoebe hugged him sincerely.

"Do you know that you're maddening?" he shook her by the shoulders.

"Pascal, you're not jealous of Rene?" she demanded gleefully. Pascal merely glared at her.

"This party has to end sometime, and when it does, we're going home and you're going to be sorry you ever looked at a beard," Pascal threatened before abandoning her to stalk off in search of a drink.

Finding a full wet bar in the billiards room, Pascal set about preparing a drink before he realized that an intimate grouping of Susan, Diana and Sloan were audibly discussing himself and Phoebe, as they lounged upon a set of high backed leather furniture off to one side of the pool table.

"So, are they into it or not?" Diana wanted to know.

"Phoebe is for certain. Not sure about Pascal," said Sloan.

"How do you know she is?" asked Susan, while Pascal also strained to hear the answer with mounting indignation.

"She told Pamela," Sloan replied.

"God, he's handsome," Susan mused, which pleased Pascal no end but reminded him that he ought to withdraw before he was noticed. And yet he longed to hear more about Phoebe. "Why don't we kidnap him for a couple of hours and use him for our pleasure?" the mischievous little blonde suggested to her dark haired friend. Diana laughed while Pascal bristled.

"Susan, behave yourself," Sloan scolded. "They're practically newlyweds and madly jealous of each other."

Pascal couldn't disagree with this assessment, but disliked being discussed in this way. Besides, the idea of being swarmed over by the two perfect New York beauties was not an unpleasant one. He wished Sloan would not discourage the girls quite so firmly.

Slipping back out of the room, Pascal went out to his car for his camera and began to traverse the mansion, snapping candid portraits of the Doll's House cast and Anthony Newton's guests.

Isolating Susan and Diana in a private room was not difficult, for they were excited by the idea of modeling for Pascal. Susan wore a black velvet suit and Diana a fitted dress of white winter wool, her shiny sable pageboy counter pointed by Susan's waist length blonde mane. They playfully posed in each other's arms. While Pascal was reloading the girls began to question and tease him.

"Your wife is glorious," Diana told him, "is she by any chance bi?"

"I never asked her," he coolly replied, a bit surprised. "Why? Are you?"

"Oh no!" Diana replied, pillowing her head against Susan's small rounded bosom and locking her arms around her blonde friend's tiny waist.

"Isn't she bad?" Susan asked Pascal as she arranged the folds of Diana's dress to expose more sheer-hosed leg for the camera.

"You're both bad," he declared, taking several shots of the new pose from different focal lengths. Susan and Diana exchanged a look. Now Susan pulled Diana closer against her and pulled up her skirt in back to reveal the brunette's stocking tops, white lace garter belt and panties.

"That's perfect," he told them. "But don't move until I tell you to."

"Too bad we didn't get to see any of Phoebe's underpinnings when she got her spanking on stage," Susan casually lamented. "But it was an exquisite moment all the same."

Pascal merely grunted in response, then said, "Okay, new pose."

Susan repositioned Diana on her knees on the loveseat, her back to Pascal, then made her lean on her elbows, and look over one shoulder with her bottom thrust out. Susan pulled up Diana's skirt again to expose her submissive's pantied bottom completely, then took the brunette by the waist as though she might either spank or caress her bottom.

"How's this, Mr. Robbins?" asked Susan ingenuously.

"Great." He took a few shots. "Okay, now take her by the earlobe," he instructed, because this was what he felt like doing to his annoying wife.

The pretty posing continued until Pascal had shot another roll.

"Thanks, girls," he told them, while Diana lit both his and Susan's cigarettes.

"May we see the proof sheets when they're ready?" Susan asked.

"Certainly," he agreed, charmed with their appreciation for fine photography.

"And now you have to drink with us," said Susan before ordering Diana to go and bring them champagne.

Susan and Diana were equally captivated by Pascal, who to them represented all that was adorable in the thirty-something male. They began to ply him with intimate questions.

"Do you spank you wife?" asked Susan.

"Only when I think of it," he replied quite honestly.

"Will you think of it tonight?" Diana asked.

"Well, what would you do?" he asked them, "After the liberties she granted that baked ham!"

"Ah ha!" cried Susan. "The spanking in the first act surprised you too?"

"I reeled," he declared, becoming carried away by the dramatic moment on top of all the drinking he'd done.

Pamela had just entered the room looking for Sloan. Unnoticed by the group on the sofa, the graceful brunette hovered for only a moment until she identified all three voices as well as the topic under discussion, then disappeared uneasily.

Going immediately to the music room, Pamela waited for a pause in the singing to take Phoebe aside and counsel her to seek out Pascal.

"But I was about to sing some more with Anthony," Phoebe protested.

"Do you want the two cutest girls here to devour your husband alive?" Pamela demanded, unable to forget, despite a friendly acquaintanceship with Susan Ross, how that young lady had nearly annexed Sloan earlier in the year.

"What do you mean, Pamela?"

The girls went out into the hall and Pamela quickly recounted the conversation she'd overheard.

"But, what should I do?" Phoebe asked her worldly counselor.

"Get Rene to take you for a stroll through the gallery. Laugh and talk gaily as you pass the billiards room. Pascal will notice."

Five minutes later, while Pascal was being charmed by the naughty girls from Manhattan, his wife passed the billiards room arm in arm with Rene.

Pascal rushed into the hall as they passed and called to Phoebe from the doorway.

"So there you are," he said.

"Here we are," said Phoebe.

"Why not come in here?" he asked, gesturing into the room with a bottle of champagne. Rene followed Phoebe in and was introduced to the girls, who immediately overwhelmed him with praise of his performance. This left Phoebe free to contend with her husband.

"Ready to go home now, Phoebe?"

"So soon?" she asked, with a flutter.

"It's almost one. And you must be feeling the strain of your big night by now."

"No, I feel wonderful."

"You'll feel even better once we get you out of that corset."

"Oh, I changed out of that right after the play," she smiled, thrilled that her waist had become reduced enough to appear corseted when it was not.

"Anyway, let's go home," he insisted.

"But wouldn't that seem rude to Mr. Newton?"

"Mr. Newton will understand perfectly."

"I should at least go and say good-bye," she decided, turning to leave. Pascal caught her by the arm.

"No, you shouldn't," he told her, leading her from the room. "Bye, girls."

"I really think I ought to thank Anthony," she declared, starting in the direction of the music room. Pascal yanked her back by her smooth forearm.

"You've done enough showing off for one night. We're going home now," he told her coldly, escorting her out of the house.

"Showing off?" She stopped on the stairs. "I beg your pardon! I happened to have starred in a play tonight."

"You sure did." He again caught her hand and pulled her after him.

Phoebe was about to begin arguing reflexively when she suddenly noticed him eyeing her as a cat eyes a sparrow.

"You just wait till I get you home, young lady," he promised, throwing her into the car.

"But, what did I do?" she demanded with a pounding heart.

"That's what I'd like to know. What exactly did you do with Rene on the days you rehearsed Act One?"

"I'm sure I don't know what you mean!"

Pascal merely sped home.

"I suppose you never thought of this happening," Phoebe cried triumphantly while buttoning herself into a quilted dressing gown and actually accepting a brandy from Pascal.

"What happening?"

"Me becoming someone!"

"What's this you're saying?"

"That you never expected me to be taken up by a VIP."

"And is that what's happened?"

"I should say it has. Why, only tonight Anthony Newton told me he's working on a play that has a fine part for me."

"I hope you're not getting a crush on that rich, attractive genius."

"Certainly not, my angel." Phoebe embraced her husband, but he took her by the shoulders and gave her a shake.

"Don't give me that," he took her over to the first armless chair he saw and turned her over his knee. "This is to remind you that you're married to me!" He pushed her light blue satin robe up to her waist to expose her bottom then brought his palm down hard and repeatedly upon its equally satiny surface. "I overheard your friends speculating about us tonight," he revealed between spates of smacks.

"What friends? What did they say?"

"Pamela, Sloan and those two brats from New York. They said it was a shame you didn't show your devoted husband more respect."

"Oh, darling!" she sighed.

"Hold still."

"But it hurts!"

"Oh, I'm sorry!" he exclaimed insincerely, while quickening the pace of his descending palm and pinkening the entire surface of her alabaster bottom.

"Now, get to bed," he ordered, pushing her off his lap, "and be prepared for anything!"

"What does that mean?" she wondered, shyly sitting on the edge of the bed.

"It means that I am going to look for the KY and bad luck for you if there is none."

When he returned, properly equipped, Phoebe was hiding behind a fort of Ralph Lauren pillows. "Pascal, I'm not ready for that!" she insisted, with an edge to her voice.

"Oh yes you are" he told her, closing in on Phoebe while she darted from one side of the bed to the other, still shielded by the pillows.

"Pascal, stop, you're scaring me!" she cried, as he grabbed her by the wrist and pulled her into swatting reach.

"Phoebe dear, get over the pillows," he told her firmly.

"No!"

"All right, I didn't want to have to do this, but you've forced me to take drastic measures," he told her before disappearing out of the room. Phoebe gazed after him in wonderment. When he returned an instant later, he was carrying the much caressed Random photo album. He sat on the bed beside her and throwing her one cool look first, leafed through the heavy black pages until he came to the photo of Marguerite Alexander whipping Diana Stratton.

"See her?" Pascal pointed to the enchanting twenty-one year old Diana.

"Yes," Phoebe replied cautiously.

"And her?" Pascal turned to the photo of dewy, blonde Susan Ross across the knee of Hugo Sands.

"Yes," Phoebe replied.

"You know who they are?"

"Yes, Susan and Diana, Anthony Newton's protégées from New York."

"Oh yeah?" he put the album on the marble dresser, "I say they're the protégées of anyone who orders either one of them to bend over in the right tone of voice."

"What are you saying?"

"I'm saying I overheard these two talking about how much they wanted to kidnap me and use me for their pleasure," Pascal reported with perfect veracity.

"You did?" Phoebe felt her heart lurch painfully.

"I'll bet they love being sodomized," he speculated.

"Pascal!"

"I could find out," he calmly threatened, "or you could obey me for once."

Phoebe glared at him momentarily, then gracefully disposed herself across the pillows, with her bottom uppermost.

"If it will help, you might imagine that I'm Anthony Newton about to give you a part, provided that you please me."

"How dare you! Mr. Newton isn't like that and neither am I!" she sprung up but he pushed her back into position.

"Oh, save your indignation for the stage and just do what you're told," he ordered, smacking her upturned bottom until she became breathless. "Rebellion over?" he asked.

"Yes," she mumbled.

"Technically, if you like being spanked, you ought to enjoy being sodomized," he mentioned, spreading her pink cheeks to expose her tiny, stubbornly compressed bottomhole. "Are you going to relax?" he asked in a warning tone.

"How can I?"

"I'll show you how," he returned, spreading her and spanking her anus. This treatment caused her to whimper without trying to squirm away. "Look how wet you are!" he charged, spanking her pussy as well. Unconsciously, she tilted up and opened up to him. The only word she said was, "Oh!" but she said it many times. Now he went to work spanking her smooth inner thighs and even the backs of her muscular calves, until she was the same shade of pink everywhere he spanked her. Phoebe thrashed, moaned and panted, taking every smack with mounting excitement.

Finally, when the heat was a tangible entity and her soft skin began to recoil from his unremitting hand, she cried out with some urgency, "I'm ready now!"

The sensations and lubricity produced by the spanking eased the shock of penetration. As an afterthought, he held one wrist behind her back as he took her bottom and this slight act of mastery seemed to affect her in a wonderful way. While her body felt stroked, filled and loved, her mind told her she was his personal whipping girl, with no choice but to submit to this humiliating and invasive punishment.

Normal, well-adjusted, guiltless Phoebe had no idea of why, in her innermost heart, she longed to be treated as the chattel of an insolent master, but this did not stop her from luxuriating in the pleasure the treatment provided. She gave up a climax in two minutes, the violent contractions of which soon wrung an explosive orgasm from his deeply lodged organ.

"Was it all that you expected?" she shyly asked, after they had disengaged and lay in each other's arms.

"I never felt closer to any woman before," he confided. "How about you?"

"I feel as though this were our true wedding night," she replied.

"We're in agreement for once." He tightened his arms around her.

"I wish we never had to leave Random Point."

About the Author

In Random Point, everything is linked to spanking and this is true for the author of the Shadow Lane novels as well. Eve Howard has been writing and producing spanking erotica since the 1980's, when she began freelancing for one of California's largest fetish magazine publishers. While editing *Spank Hard* magazine (as Lizzie Bennett) in 1985, she was discovered by the video producer Nu-West and offered a chance to perform in spanking videos. In 1986 she published the first Shadow Lane story and the following year formed the video production company Shadow Lane with her partner Tony Elka. The Shadow Lane novel series, originally published by Eve in serial form in her magazine *Stand Corrected*, was brought out in paperback volumes by Blue Moon books beginning in 1992. There are nine titles in the Shadow Lane series and Eve is currently working on Volume 10.

Since 1988, Eve has written, directed and produced over 140 spanking videos, the vast majority featuring the same male-spanks-female dynamic portrayed in her novels. Female-friendly and designed to make people feel good, rather than guilty, about being into spanking, Eve suggests an irreverent alternative to the all or nothing B&D subculture portrayed in such beloved classics as *The Story of O*. Many spanking fans have discovered the real life spanking scene by following the same patterns of social networking as described in the Shadow Lane novels. And for almost twenty years, Eve's company Shadow Lane has been one of the primary social organs of the real life spanking scene. She lives with her husband Tony and three cats in Las Vegas.

Reader Reviews about the Shadow Lane Series

"I've become addicted to the "Random Point" series so much that I can't wait until the next chapter. I've ordered the first two Shadow Lane volumes and have re-read them over and over. I never tire of them. Eve is the only person I know who can make an enema sexy."

"I discovered Shadow Lane about a month ago via AOL. Prior to that time I thought I could write excellent spanking erotica. Then I ordered, "The Problem with Laura." This is just a note to commend Eve Howard's spectacular talent and to say thanks for an incredible erotic experience."

"I have just completed "Return to Random Point" and decided that I had to write about how much I enjoyed it. I have not been so aroused since reading my first discipline novel many years ago, about a girl raised in England and "coming of age" as I believe they put it. More recently I have enjoyed reading Grant Andrews' My Darling Dominatrix and Ann Rice's "Beauty" series. It seems that women, though, have the right touch when it comes to writing about this subject. Eve, especially, knows how to touch that erotic nerve and bring it to a pure, raw sensuality until one feels that he/she is near bursting with lust."

"I, for one, have always loved (and by loved I mean devoured... breathlessly) Eve Howard's novelettes. To read them... especially when I was just 'coming out'... was to feel completely validated. I truly identified with each and every heroine; the feisty, sassy ones, the shy, demure ultra 'subby' ones... the young ones, and the more mature. I loved the gentle yet firm "taken in hand" nature of the romantic variety of spanking D's that Eve always incorporated into the stories. I loved that the plots were not complicated... but, feasible nonetheless. I loved the depictions of sexual escapades after many of the spanking interludes. I appreciated that the girls were cherished and adored by the affably rogue-ish gents... that the submitting was willing and desired... that it wasn't like 'rape.'

I like the settings... having grown up in New England and living here almost my whole life. I LOVED the idea of the bookstore (which I always find sexy). Then and now. I could cite many passages too, but I fear I've rambled enough. Eve was/is always my favorite spanking author."

www.ingramcontent.com/pod-product-compliance
Lightning Source LLC
Chambersburg PA
CBHW020846260626
47169CB00003B/1157